As much as he loathed himself for being forced to do it, Byrok ran.

It was a hard thing for him, and not just because the dagger that was still protruding from his thigh slowed his gait. To run from battle was shameful. But Byrok knew he had a higher duty to perform—the Burning Blade had returned, only this time they were humans. And *all* the attackers, not just the two he'd noticed before, wore that flaming sword image somewhere on them: a necklace, a tattoo, *something*.

This was information that needed to get back to Thrall.

So Byrok ran.

Then he stumbled. His left leg refused to lift as it was supposed to—but his right leg continued to run, and so he crashed to the ground, high grass and dirt getting in his nose and mouth and eye.

"Must . . . get . . . up . . ."

"You ain't goin' nowhere, monster." Byrok could hear the voice, hear the humans' footfalls, and then feel the pressure when two of them sat on his back, immobilizing him. " 'Cause, here's the thing—your time is over. Orcs don't belong in this world, and so we're gonna take you out of it. Got me?"

Byrok managed the effort of lifting his head so he could see two of the humans. He spat at them.

The humans just laughed. "Let's do it, boys. *Galtak Ered'nash!*"

The other five all replied in kind: *"Galtak Ered'nash!"*

WORLD OF WARCRAFT®

CYCLE OF HATRED

KEITH R.A. DeCANDIDO

POCKET STAR BOOKS

New York   London   Toronto   Sydney

An *Original* Publication of POCKET BOOKS

A Pocket Star Book published by
POCKET BOOKS, a division of Simon & Schuster, Inc.
1230 Avenue of the Americas, New York, NY 10020

This book is a work of fiction. Names, characters, places and incidents are products of the author's imagination or are used fictitiously. Any resemblance to actual events or locales or persons, living or dead, is entirely coincidental.

ISBN-13: 978-0-7434-7136-7
ISBN-10:   0-7434-7136-9

This Pocket Star Books paperback edition February 2006

10   9

POCKET STAR BOOKS and colophon are registered trademarks of Simon & Schuster, Inc.

Cover art by Glenn Rane

Manufactured in the United States of America

For information regarding special discounts for bulk purchases, please contact Simon & Schuster Special Sales at 1-800-456-6798 or business@simonandschuster.com.

To GraceAnne Andreassi DeCandido,

Helga Borck, Ursula K. Le Guin,

Constance Hassett, Joanne Dobson,

and all the other women who taught me so much

ACKNOWLEDGMENTS

Primary thanks must go to Blizzard Games guru Chris Metzen, whose contributions to everything *Warcraft* cannot be understated. Our phone conversations and e-mail exchanges were tremendously fruitful and full of an amazing creative energy.

Secondary thanks go to Marco Palmieri, my editor at Pocket Books, and his boss Scott Shannon, who both thought this would be a good idea; and to Lucienne Diver, my magnificent agent.

Tertiary thanks to the other *Warcraft* novelists, Richard Knaak, Jeff Grubb, and Christie Golden. In particular, Jeff's *The Last Guardian* and Christie's *Lord of the Clans* were very helpful with the characterizations of Aegwynn and Thrall, respectively.

Gratitude also to: the Malibu Gang, the Elitist Bastards, Novelscribes, Inkwell, and all the other mailing lists that keep my sanity by making me insane; CITH and CGAG; the folks at Palombo who put up with me; *Kyoshi* Paul and the rest of the good folks at the dojo; and, as ever, the forebearance of those that live with me, both human and feline, for all the continued support.

HISTORIAN'S NOTE

This novel takes place one year prior to *World of Warcraft*. It is three years after the invasion by the Burning Legion and their defeat by the combined forces of the orcs, humans, and night elves *(Warcraft 3: Reign of Chaos* and *Warcraft 3X: The Frozen Throne)*.

ONE

Erik had been cleaning ale off the demon skull mounted behind the bar when the stranger walked in.

The Demonsbane Inn and Tavern didn't usually get much by way of tourists. Rare was the day when Erik didn't know the face of one of his patrons. More common was when he didn't know their names—he only remembered their faces due to repeated exposure. Erik didn't much care *who* came into his tavern, as long as they had coin and a thirst.

Sitting down at a table, the stranger seemed to be either waiting for something or looking for something. He wasn't looking at the dark wooden walls—though you could barely see them, seeing as how the Demonsbane had no windows and illumination only from a couple of torches—or at the small round wooden tables and stools that festooned the floor. Erik never bothered to arrange the tables in any particular pattern, since folks would just go and move them around to suit themselves anyhow.

After a minute, the stranger got up and walked up to the wooden bar. "I'm trying to get some table service."

"Don't have none," Erik said. He never saw the sense in paying good money for waiters. If folks wanted a drink, they could walk up to the bar. If they were too drunk to walk up to the bar, he didn't want them to drink anymore anyhow, since folks who were that drunk were like to start fights. Erik ran a quiet tavern.

The stranger plunked a silver piece on the bar and asked, "What's the most expensive drink you have there?"

"That'd be the boar's grog from the north. Orcs make it, ferment it in—"

The stranger's nose wrinkled. "No—no orc drink."

Erik shrugged. People had weird considerations when it came to alcohol. He'd seen folks argue about the relative merits of beer versus corn whiskey with more intensity than they brought to political or religious disagreements. If this gentleman didn't like orc drinks, that wasn't Erik's lookout. "Got corn whiskey— fresh batch made last month."

"Sold." The stranger smacked his hand on the wooden bar, disturbing some of the nut shells, berry seeds, and other detritus that had gathered there. Erik only cleaned the bar about once a year or so—unlike the demon skull, no one could really see the bar, and he never saw the need to clean a surface that wasn't visible.

One of the regulars, a soldier who always drank the

grog, turned to look at the stranger. "Mind tellin' me what you got against orc booze?"

The stranger shrugged while Erik pulled the glass bottle of corn whiskey off the shelf and poured some of its contents into a mug that was mostly clean.

"I have nothing against orc drink, good sir—it's orcs themselves I have issue with." The stranger held out a hand. "My name is Margoz. I'm a fisherman by trade, and I have to say that I'm not well pleased with how my nets have filled up this season."

Not bothering to shake the hand or introduce himself, the soldier said, "All that tells me is you ain't no good as a fisherman."

Lowering his hand upon realizing that the soldier wasn't feeling friendly, Margoz took his corn whiskey instead. "I'm a fine fisherman, sir—I thrived in Kul Tiras, before circumstances forced me to move here."

On the other side of Margoz sat a merchant who sputtered into his ale. "Circumstances. Right. Got conscripted to fight the Burning Legion, did you?"

Margoz nodded. "As I'm sure many were. I tried to make a new life for myself here in Theramore—but how can I, with the damned greenskins taking all the good fishing waters for themselves?"

Erik found himself nodding in agreement with the first half of Margoz's statement, if not the second. He himself had come to Theramore after the Burning Legion was driven off—not to fight, as the fighting was over by the time he made the journey, but to claim his inheritance. Erik's brother Olaf had fought against the Legion and died, leaving Erik enough coin to build the tavern Olaf had dreamed of opening after he finished his service. In addition to the money, Erik was bequeathed the skull of a demon that Olaf had slain in combat. Erik had never particularly wanted to run a tavern, but he'd never particularly wanted to do anything else, so he opened the Demonsbane in honor of his brother. He figured, rightly, that the community of humans in Theramore would gravitate toward a place with a name that symbolized the driving off of demons that led to the city-state's formation.

"I ain't standin' for this," the soldier said. "You fought in the war, fisherman—you know what the orcs did for us."

"What they *did* for us is not what distresses me, good sir," Margoz said, "but rather what they are doing *to* us now."

"They get the best of everything." This was the boat captain at one of the tables behind the soldier. "Up Ratchet way, them goblins always favor orcs for repairs or dock space. Last month, I had to wait half a day 'fore they'd let me dock my skiff, but some orc boat come by two hour after me, and got a spot right off."

Turning to face the captain, the soldier said, "Then go somewhere other than Ratchet."

"T'ain't always an option," the captain said with a sneer.

" 'S not like they always *need* the repairin', neither,"

the man with the captain—Erik thought it might have been his first mate, since they dressed similarly—said. "They got oaks up in mountains above Orgrimmar, be makin' their ships from them. What we got? Weak spruce is all. They hoard 'em, they do, keepin' all the good wood. Our boats'll be leakin' all over thanks to the marshy garbage we gotta work with."

Several other voices muttered in agreement with this sentiment.

"So you'd all like it better if the orcs weren't around?" The soldier slammed his fist on the bar. "Without them, we'd be demon-food, and that's a fact."

"I don't think anyone's denying that." Margoz sipped from his whiskey mug. "Still, there does seem to be an unequal distribution of resources."

"Orcs used to be slaves, you know." This was someone else at the bar whom Erik couldn't see from where he was standing. "To humans, and to the Burning Legion, if you think about it. Can't blame 'em for wanting to take everything they can now."

"I can if they're takin' it away from *us*," the captain said.

The merchant nodded. "You know, they're not *from* here. They came from some other world, and the Burning Legion brought 'em here."

The first mate muttered, "Maybe they oughta go back where they came."

"Makes you wonder what Lady Proudmoore was thinking," Margoz said.

Erik frowned. At those words, the tavern suddenly got rather quiet. Lots of people had been muttering assent or disagreement, either with the sentiments expressed or the people expressing them.

But as soon as Margoz mentioned Jaina Proudmoore—worse, mentioned her in a disparaging manner—the place got quiet.

Too quiet. In the three years Erik had been a tavern owner, he learned that there were two times when you expected a fight to break out: when the place got too loud, and when it got too quiet. And the latter times usually brought on the really nasty fights.

Another soldier stood up next to the first one—this one was wider in the shoulders, and he didn't talk much, but when he did, it was in a booming voice that made the demon skull behind the bar rattle on its mount. "Don't nobody talk bad 'bout Lady Proudmoore 'less he wants to be livin' without teeth."

Swallowing audibly, Margoz quickly said, "I would never dream of speaking of our leader in anything but reverent tones, good sir, I promise." He gulped down more of the corn whiskey than it was advisable to drink in one sip, which caused his eyes to greatly widen. He shook his head a few times.

"Lady Proudmoore's been very good to us," the merchant said. "After we drove back the Burning Legion, she made us into a *community*. Your complaints are fair, Margoz, but none of it can be laid at the lady's feet. I've met a few wizards in my day, and most of 'em aren't fit to be scrapings off my sandals. But the lady's a good one, and you'll find no support for disparagements of her."

"It was never my intent to disparage, good sir," Margoz said, still sounding a bit shaky from his ill-advised gulp of corn whiskey. "But one must wonder why no trade agreements have been made to obtain this superior wood that these fine gentlemen have mentioned." He looked thoughtful for a second. "Perhaps she has tried, but the orcs would not permit it."

The captain swallowed a gulp of his ale, then said, "Perhaps them orcs told her to leave Northwatch."

"We *should* leave Northwatch," the merchant said. "The Barrens are neutral territory, that was agreed to from the beginning."

The soldier stiffened. "You're crazy if you think we're givin' *that* up."

Margoz said, "That *is* where the orcs fought Admiral Proudmoore."

"Yes, an embarrassment. As fine a leader as Lady Proudmoore is, that's how much of an idiot her father was." The merchant shook his head. "That entire sordid incident should be put out of our heads. But it won't be as long as—"

The captain interrupted. "If'n you ask me, we need to expand *beyond* Northwatch."

Sounding annoyed—though whether at the interruption or the sentiment, Erik neither knew nor cared—the merchant said, "Are you mad?"

"Are you? The orcs're squeezin' us out! They're all over the blessed continent, and we've got Theramore. It's been three year since the Burning Legion was sent off. Don't we deserve better than to be lower class in our own land—to be confined to one cesspool of a city-state?"

"Theramore is as fine a city as you will see in human lands." The soldier spoke the words with a defensive pride, only to continue in a more resigned tone. "But it is true that the orcs have greater territory. That is why Northwatch is essential—it allows us to maintain a defense beyond the walls of Theramore."

"Besides," the first mate said with a laugh into his ale mug, "the orcs don't like us there. That's reason enough to keep it, y'ask me."

"Nobody asked you," the merchant said snidely.

The other man at the bar—Erik had wandered down-bar a bit, and now saw that it was that bookkeeper who worked the docks—said, "Maybe someone should. The orcs act as if they own Kalimdor, and we're just visiting. But this is our home, too, and it's time we acted like it. Orcs aren't humans, aren't even *from* this world. What right do they have to dictate how we live our lives?"

"They have the right to live *their* lives, don't they?" the merchant asked.

Nodding, the soldier said, "I'd say they earned that when they fought the Burning Legion. Weren't for them . . ." He gulped down the remainder of his wine, then slid the mug toward Erik. "Get me an ale."

Erik hesitated. He had already started reaching for the grog bottle. This soldier had been coming into the Demonsbane ever since Erik opened the place, and he'd never drunk anything save grog.

But that three-year-long patronage had earned him the right not to be questioned. Besides, as long as he was paying, he could drink soapy water for all Erik cared.

"Fact is," the captain said, "this is our world, by right of birth. Them orcs are just guests in our home, and it's high time they started *actin'* like it!"

The conversation went on from there. Erik served a few more drinks, tossed a few mugs into the basin to be cleaned later, and only after he gave the merchant another ale did he realize that Margoz, who started the whole conversation, had left.

He hadn't even left a tip. Erik shook his head in disgust, the fisherman's name already falling out of his head.

But he'd remember the face. And probably spit in the bastard's drink next time he came in—having only one drink and then starting trouble. Erik hated troublemakers like that in his place. Just hated it.

More people started complaining about the orcs. One person—the bruiser next to the soldier—slammed his ale mug on the bar so hard that it spattered his drink on the demon skull. Sighing, Erik grabbed a rag and wiped it off.

There was a time when Margoz would have been too scared to walk the darkened streets of Theramore alone.

True, crime was not a major concern in so closed a community as Theramore—everyone knew most everyone else, and if they didn't, they knew someone else who did—so criminal acts were rare enough. Those that were committed were generally punished quickly and brutally by Lady Proudmoore's soldiers.

Still, Margoz had always been small and weak, and the big and strong tended to prey on the small and weak, so Margoz generally avoided walking around alone at night. You never knew what big and strong person was lurking to show how big and strong he was by beating up on a lesser target. Many times, Margoz had been that target. He soon learned that it was best to do what they said and make them happy in order to avoid the violence.

But Margoz no longer had that fear. Or any other kind of fear. Now he had a patron. True, Margoz had to do his bidding, also, but this time the reward was power and wealth. In the old days, the reward was not being beaten within an inch of his life. Maybe it was exchanging one type of gut-crippling fear for another, but Margoz thought this was working out better for him.

A salty breeze wafted through the air, blowing in off the port. Margoz inhaled deeply, the scent of the water invigorating him. He spoke at least partly true in the Demonsbane: he was a fisherman, though never a particularly successful one. However, he did not fight against the Burning Legion as he claimed, but instead came here after they'd been driven back. He'd hoped to have more opportunities here than he'd had at Kul Tiras. It wasn't *his* fault that the nets were substandard—they were all he could afford, but tell the dock authority *that* and see where it got you.

Where it got him, mostly, was beaten up.

So he came to Kalimdor, following the rush of people hoping to provide services for the humans who lived there under Lady Proudmoore. But Margoz hadn't been the only fisherman to ply his trade, nor was he anywhere near the best.

Before his patron arrived, Margoz was close to destitute. He wasn't even catching enough to feed himself, much less sell, and he was seriously considering just grabbing his boat's anchor and jumping off the side with it. Put himself out of his misery.

But then his patron arrived, and everything got better.

Margoz soon arrived at his modest apartment. His patron hadn't let him move to better accommodations, despite his pleading—the patron called it whining, and unseemly—regarding the lack of good ventilation, the poor furnishings, and the rats. But his patron assured him that such a sudden change in his status would draw attention, and for now, he was to remain unnoticed.

Until tonight, when he was instructed to go to the Demonsbane and start sowing anti-orc sentiments. In the old days, he never would have dared to set foot in such a place. The types of people who liked to beat him up usually congregated in large groups in taverns, and he preferred to avoid them for that reason.

Or, rather, used to prefer to avoid them.

He entered his room. A pallet that was no thinner than a slice of bread; a burlap sheet that itched so much he only used it when the winter got particularly cold, and even then it was a difficult choice; a lantern; and precious little else. A rat scurried across into one of the many cracks in the wall.

Sighing, he knew what needed to be done next. Besides the inability to move to better quarters, the thing Margoz hated most about his dealings with his patron was the odor he carried with him afterwards. It was some kind of side effect of the magic at his patron's command, but whatever the reason, it annoyed Margoz.

Still, it was worth it for the power. And the ability to walk the streets and drink in the Demonsbane without fear of physical reprisal.

Shoving his hand past his collar to reach under his shirt, Margoz pulled out the necklace with the silver pendant shaped like a sword afire. Clutching the sword so tightly that he felt the edges dig into his palm, he spoke the words whose meaning he'd never learned, but which filled him with an unspeakable dread every time he said them: *"Galtak Ered'nash. Ered'nash ban galar. Ered'nash havik yrthog. Galtak Ered'nash."*

The stink of sulfur started to permeate the small room. This was the part Margoz hated.

Galtak Ered'nash. **You have done as I commanded?**

"Yes, sir." Margoz was embarrassed to realize that his voice was getting squeaky. Clearing his throat, he tried to deepen his tone. "I did as you asked. As soon as I mentioned difficulties with the orcs, virtually the entire tavern joined in."

Virtually?

Margoz didn't like the threat implied in that one-word question. "One man was a holdout, but the others were ganging up on him to a certain degree. Provided a focus for their ire, really."

Perhaps. You have done well.

That came as a huge relief. "Thank you, sir, thank you. I am glad to have been of service." He hesitated. "If I may, sir, might now be a good time to once again broach the subject of improved accommodations? You might have noticed the rat that—"

You have served us. You will be rewarded.

"So you've said, sir, but—well, I was hoping a reward would come soon." He decided to take advantage of his lifelong fears. "I was in grave danger this evening, you know. Walking alone near the docks can be—"

You will come to no harm as long as you serve. You need never walk with fear again, Margoz.

"Of—of course. I simply—"

You simply wish to live the life you have never been permitted to live. That is an understandable concern. Be patient, Margoz. Your reward will come in due time.

The sulfur stench started to abate. "Thank you, sir. *Galtak Ered'nash!*"

Dimly, the patron's voice said, *Galtak Ered'nash.* Then all was quiet in Margoz's apartment once again.

A bang came on the wall, followed by the muffled voice of his neighbor. "Stop yelling in there! We're tryin' to sleep!"

Once, such importunings would have had Margoz cowering in fear. Today, he simply ignored them and lay down on his pallet, hoping the smell wouldn't keep him from sleeping.

TWO

What I don't get is, what's the *point* of fog?"
Captain Bolik, master of the orc trading
vessel *Orgath'ar,* knew he would regret the
words even as he found himself almost compelled to respond to his batman's statement. "Does it *have* to have a
point?"

Rabin shook his head as he continued his cleaning of
the captain's tusks. It was not a habit every orc indulged
in, but Bolik felt that it was his duty as captain of the *Orgath'ar* to present himself in the best manner possible.
Orcs were a noble people, ripped from their homes and
enslaved, both by demons and by humans. Enslaved orcs
had always been filthy and unkempt. As a free orc living
in Durotar under the benign rule of the great warrior
Thrall, Bolik felt it was important to look as little like the
slaves of old as possible. That meant grooming, as alien
a concept as that might have been to most orcs, and it
was something he expected in his crew as well.

Certainly it was true of Rabin, who had taken to the captain's instructions far better than most of *Orgath'ar*'s crew. Rabin kept his eyebrows trimmed, his tusks and teeth cleaned, his nails polished and sharp, and kept decoration to a tasteful minimum—just a nose ring and a tattoo.

In answer to Bolik's question, Rabin said, "Well, everything in the world serves *some* purpose, don't it, sir? I mean, the water, it's there to be givin' us fish to eat and a way of travelin' by boat. The air's there to be givin' us something to breathe. The ground gives us food, too, not to mention somethin' to build our homes on. We're makin' boats with what the trees give us. Even rain and snow—they're givin' us water we can drink, unlike the sea. All that *means* something."

Rabin turned his attention to sharpening Bolik's nails, and so Bolik leaned back. His stool was situated near the cabin bulkhead, so he leaned against that. "But fog means nothing?"

"All it does, really, is get in the way without givin' us nothin'."

Bolik smiled, his freshly cleaned teeth shining in the cabin's dim lantern-provided illumination. The porthole provided none such, thanks to the very fog that Rabin was now complaining about. The captain asked, "But snow and rain get in the way, too."

"True enough, Captain, true enough." Rabin finished sharpening the thumb and moved on to the other fingers. "But, like I said, snow and rain got themselves a greater purpose. Even if they do get in the way, leastaways there's a benefit to be makin' up for it. But tell me, sir, what does the fog do to make up for it? It keeps us from seein' where we goin', and don't give us nothing back."

"Perhaps." Bolik regarded his batman. "Or perhaps we simply haven't learned its benefit yet. After all, there was a time when we did not know that snow was simply frozen rain. The orcs then saw snow only as the same kind of problem that you now see fog as. Eventually, its true purpose—as you said, to provide us with water to drink during the colder seasons—was learned. So it is not the fault of the fog, but ours for not yet seeing the truth. And that is as it should be. The world tells us what we need to know when we are ready to know it and not before. That is the way of things."

Rabin considered the captain's words as he finished sharpening and started buffing. "I suppose that might be so. But that don't do us much good today, though, does it, sir?"

"No, it does not. How is the crew dealing with it?"

"As well as can be, I suppose," Rabin said with a shrug. "Lookout says he can't see the tusks in front of his face from up there."

Bolik frowned. The rocking of the boat had been fairly constant, but now it seemed to bounce a bit more. That usually meant they were being affected by the wake of another vessel.

Rising from the stool while Rabin was in mid-sharpen, Bolik said, "We'll finish this later, Rabin."

Getting up off his knees, Rabin nodded his head. "Very well, Captain."

Bolik grabbed his father's mace and exited his cabin into the narrow corridor beyond. *Orgath'ar*—which Bolik had named after Orgath, his noble father and the original owner of the mace, who died fighting the Burning Legion—had been built by goblins, since he wanted only the best. The shipbuilder, a sharp old goblin named Leyds, had assured Bolik that he would make the corridors extra wide to accommodate orcs' greater girth. Unfortunately, the short goblin's notions of "extra wide" were less generous than Bolik's, so the captain was barely able to squeeze his massive frame through to the staircase that led to the deck.

As he walked up the stairs, he saw his first mate, Kag, stop himself from coming down. "I was just coming to see you, sir." Kag smiled, his long tusks almost poking his eyes. "Should've known you'd feel the change."

Bolik chuckled as he came up to the deck. As soon as he arrived, he regretted not calling Kag back downstairs to meet him. The fog was almost thick enough to cut with his sword. He knew *Orgath'ar* well enough to walk to the edge of the deck without being able to see where he was going, but now that was the *only* way to get there. Kag followed, standing practically nose to nose with the captain so they could see each other.

Realizing that he wasn't going to be able to see any other ships—indeed, he barely had any empirical evidence that they were actually in a body of water, since he could hardly see *that*—he turned to his first mate. "What is it?"

Kag shook his head. "Hard to say. Lookout can't see much. He's caught glimpses of a ship, but sometimes he thinks it's one of the Theramore military convoys— other times, he says he looks nothing like any regular human *or* orc boat."

"What do you think?"

Without hesitating, Kag said, "Lookout wouldn't say if he wasn't sure. If he says he saw Theramore military, then says something else, that means he saw something different the first time. I think it's two ships. Besides, the wake's enough for two, or for one going 'round in circles. This fog, one's as like as the other."

Bolik nodded his agreement. Their lookout, Vak, could look at two specks on the horizon and tell you which was the fishing boat and which the troop carrier. Probably tell you whether or not the fishing boat was built by gnomes or humans, too, and whether the troop carrier was made before or after the Burning Legion's invasion. "Three ships this close is asking for trouble. We may need to sound the horn. Get—"

"Ship ho!"

Casting his glance up the mast, Bolik tried to see Vak, but the mast above his head was swallowed by fog. Vak's voice carried down from what humans called the "crow's nest," for reasons Bolik never understood—he knew that a crow was a type of bird, but he wasn't sure what its nest had to do with a lookout post—but the captain could not see him.

Kag called up. "What do you see?"

"Ship approaching! Humans! Not flying no colors I can see!"

"What about the military ship?"

"Can't see 'em now, but caught 'em a second ago! Runnin' parallel now!"

Bolik didn't like this. A human ship flying no colors usually meant pirates. It might not have—flying colors was almost pointless in fog like this—and they might simply have been unable to see the orc ship. Bolik wasn't about to risk the possibility—or his cargo. If the crates in his hold weren't safely delivered to Razor Hill, Bolik didn't get paid, which meant the crew didn't get paid. Days the crew lost wages were never good days to be a shipmaster.

"Sound the horn. And put guards on the cargo hold."

Kag nodded. "Yes, sir."

"Harpoons!"

At Vak's cry, Bolik cursed. Harpoons meant only one of two things. One was that the other ship had mistaken *Orgath'ar* for a large seafaring creature such as a whale or a sea serpent. The other was that they were pirates and the harpoons were attached to boarding lines.

Since sea serpents and whales didn't migrate this far north as a general rule, Bolik felt safe in assuming it was the latter.

The harpoons slammed into the deck, the side of the

staircase that led belowdecks, and other places Bolik couldn't see in the fog. Then the lines that were attached to them went taut.

"Prepare for boarders!" Kag cried.

Bolik heard a voice say, "Cut the lines!"

The sound of a fist hitting flesh was followed by Kag saying, "Don't be a fool! Swords can't cut through those ropes, and you'll leave yourself open."

Any other conversation was cut short by the sudden arrival of the very boarders in question, appearing as if by magic in the fog. They were human, Bolik saw, and not in any kind of military uniform. Beyond that, Bolik wasn't sure what they were wearing—humans' fascination with outerwear beyond what was absolutely necessary was something that had always baffled Bolik. He knew what Lady Proudmoore's military wore, but that was it.

"Kill the pirates!" Bolik cried, but his crew needed no such prompting. The battle was joined. Bolik lifted his father's mace in his right hand and swung it at the closest human, who ducked out of the way, then lunged with his sword.

Bolik parried the sword with his left arm, but by the time he was able to whirl the mace around his head for a second strike, the human had gotten his sword up to block the mace. However, when he leaned in to do so, the human moved his stomach closer to Bolik, making it easy for the orc captain to punch his foe with his fist. Doubling over in pain and coughing, the human collapsed to the deck, and Bolik brought his mace down on the back of the human's neck.

Two more then leapt in front of Bolik, no doubt expecting him to cower at two-to-one odds. But Bolik was made of sterner stuff. Though born a slave in this world, he had been freed by Thrall, and swore he would never cower before a human again. He had fought alongside them, true, but never would he bow to one as an inferior.

Nor to two who came at him with swords.

The pirate to his left attacked with his blade—a curved one of a type Bolik had seen only once before—while the one on his right swung two shorter swords. Bolik blocked the curved blade with his left arm, though this time the edge bit into his forearm, while using the mace to deflect one of the two short swords. The other short sword missed Bolik's chest by a hair.

Although the movement sent searing pain through his left arm, Bolik brought the limb swiftly downward, the blade still stuck in it. His superior strength and leverage meant that the foe on his left was now disarmed, his weapon lodged in Bolik's own flesh. Kicking at the pirate to his right, Bolik grabbed the head of the one on his left and pushed down, forcing the pirate to his knees.

The one with the short swords flailed as he stumbled to the deck, managing to avoid a leg-breaking kick, but unable to keep his balance in the bargain.

Bolik, still with his massive left hand on the head of the curved-sword-holding pirate, cast that fool aside.

The human's head hit the mast with a satisfying thud.

However, that move gave the other one a chance to regain his footing. Even as he lunged with his two tiny swords, Bolik leaned back and to his right, straightened his right arm behind him, then swung the mace over his head, bringing it smashing down on the human's skull, killing him instantly.

"Vak!" Bolik yelled up the mast as he removed the curved sword from his arm and tossed it to the deck next to its insensate owner. "Sound the horn!" The pirates likely didn't know the orcish tongue, and so wouldn't expect it when the foghorn went off.

Seconds later, an ear-splitting noise filled the air. Bolik was prepared for the sound that felt as if it vibrated his very bones, as were his crew, he assumed—he couldn't really see most of them.

The humans that Bolik could see were caught off guard, however, which Bolik had counted on. The orcs that Bolik could see pressed their advantage. Bolik himself started twirling his mace over his head until he found a good target. His father's weapon slammed into the shoulder of a nearby pirate, who fell to the floor, screaming in agony.

Bolik heard a human voice yell a word in the human tongue that he was fairly sure meant "retreat," a guess that was proven accurate as the pirates started to climb the ropes back to their vessel. Bolik saw Kag slice off the leg of one of the retreaters, causing the victim to fall into the Great Sea.

Kag turned to Bolik. "Do we give chase?"

Shaking his head, Bolik said, "No. Let them go." There was little point in trying to chase a ship in this be-damned fog. "Check the cargo."

Nodding acknowledgment, Kag ran off to the hold entry, his footfalls echoing on the deck.

Gazing upward, Bolik said, "Lookout, what about the human ship?"

"They didn't move," Vak said, "until after we sounded fog. Then they moved off. Don't see 'em now."

Bolik's fists tightened, his right hand gripping the handle of his father's mace so hard, he thought it might break. The humans were their allies. If some of Lady Proudmoore's precious soldiers were nearby, why did they not assist when brigands boarded *Orgath'ar*?

"Sir," Kag said, returning alongside Forx, the warrior in charge of guarding the cargo, "one of the crates was smashed. Another was thrown overboard by one of the humans to cover his retreat."

Forx added, "They sent most o' their men to the hold. We drove 'em back good, we did, sir. They'd'a taken it all otherwise."

"You did well, Forx. And you will be rewarded." Bolik knew his words would have meaning. Two crates lost meant twenty percent of their cargo was useless, which meant a twenty percent reduction in wages. Bolik put a hand on Forx's shoulder. "You shall all receive the same cut you would have if all the cargo came intact—the difference will come out of my own share."

Kag's eyes grew wide. "You honor us all, Captain."

"Not at all—you defended my ship. You won't be penalized for that."

Forx smiled. "I'll inform your warriors, sir."

Bolik turned to Kag as Forx went off. "Assess damage, dump any human bodies into the sea, and put us back on course." He took a breath, then blew it out through his tusks. "And when we return, I want a messenger found. Thrall must be informed of this right away."

Nodding, Kag said, "Yes, Captain."

Staring into the fog that had allowed the pirates to get so close for their attack, Bolik thought back on Rabin's words, and decided that no use they could get from fog would be worth this. . . .

THREE

Lady Jaina Proudmoore stood atop the butte on Razor Hill, gazing out over the land where she helped form the most unlikely alliance in the history of the world.

Razor Hill was orc territory, of course, but Jaina and Thrall had agreed that, given her abilities, it was best for their meetings to happen on orc land, where Thrall generally was. For Jaina's part, her magic allowed her to go wherever she wished in an instant.

In truth, when the summons had come from Thrall, it had come as a relief. Jaina's entire adult life, it seemed, consisted of going from one crisis to another. She had fought demons and orcs and warlords, and had the fate of the world in her small hands more than once.

She once was the lover of Arthas, when he was a noble warrior, but he had been corrupted, was now the Lich King of the Scourge, the cruelest warlord in a world that had seen its fair share of them. Some day, she knew, she would have to face him in battle. Medivh, the Sargeras-cursed wizard who had seemingly doomed humanity by letting demons and orcs overrun this world, became a staunch ally who convinced Jaina and Thrall to unite their people with the night elves against the Burning Legion.

After that, when the humans built Theramore as their new home on Kalimdor, Jaina had thought that things would calm down. But things were never calm when one ruled, even in times of peace, and she found that the day-to-day running of Theramore almost made her long for the days when she was fighting for her life.

Almost, but not quite. In truth, she had few regrets—but she also grabbed the opportunity for a respite like a desert traveler grabbing a water flask.

Standing at one edge of the butte, she looked far down on the small orc village at the base of the hills. Well-defended huts dotted the harsh brown landscape. Even in times of peace, the orcs made sure their homes would not be taken. A few orcs walked between the huts, greeting each other, some pausing to speak. Jaina couldn't help but smile at such quotidian simplicity.

Then she heard the low, steady rumble that heralded the arrival of Thrall's airship. Turning around, she saw the massive dirigible approach. As it grew closer, she saw that only Thrall stood in the undercarriage that was carried along beneath the massive hot-air-filled canvas that propelled the machine through the air. Said canvas was decorated with a variety of symbols, some of which Jaina recognized as pictographs from an old version of the orc language. One, she knew, was the symbol of Thrall's family, the Frostwolf clan. That was the main thing that differentiated orc airships from the ones Jaina's people used—the airships that Theramore had rented from the goblins were more nondescript affairs. Jaina wondered if the orcs' way might not be better—to imbue their non-living transports with personalities akin to that of living mounts.

In the past, when they'd met on the butte, Thrall had at least brought a guard or two. That he was traveling alone now concerned Jaina greatly.

As the airship approached, Thrall pulled some levers, and the dirigible slowed, finally coming to a hover over the butte. Pulling one final lever, Thrall lowered a rope ladder and climbed down. Like most orcs, Thrall had green skin and black hair, the latter braided and draped over his shoulders. The black plate armor with bronze trim he wore belonged to Orgrim Doomhammer, Thrall's mentor and the man for whom Durotar's capital city had been named. Strapped to his back was Orgrim's weapon, from which he derived his last name: the Doomhammer, a two-handed weapon that Jaina had seen Thrall use in battle. The blood of many a demon had been shed with that great hammer.

What stood out about Thrall most, though, were his blue eyes, a color rarely found in orcs. They bespoke both his intelligence and his kindness.

Three years ago, while both Theramore and the

cities of Durotar were being built, Jaina had given Thrall a magical talisman: a small stone carved in the shape of one of the old *Tirisfalen* runes. Jaina had its twin in her own possession. Thrall needed only to hold it and think of her, and Jaina's talisman would glow; the reverse also held true. If they wished to meet in secret, to discuss issues that affected one or the other, or both, of their people away from the politics of their positions as leaders—or if they simply wished to talk as old friends and comrades—all they had to do was activate the talisman. Jaina would then teleport to the butte, and Thrall would come by airship, since the butte was inaccessible any other way.

"It is good to see you, my friend," Jaina said with a warm smile. And she meant it. In all her life, she'd known no one as honorable and dependable as the orc. Once, she would have numbered her father and Arthas among those. But Admiral Proudmoore insisted on attacking the orcs at Kalimdor, refusing to believe his own daughter when she said that the orcs were as much victims of the Burning Legion as humans were, and were *not* evil. Like so many people Jaina had known, Admiral Proudmoore was unable to accept that the world was different from the way it was when he was younger, and fought against any alteration to it. That included the presence of orcs, and Jaina had been put in the terrible position of betraying her own father to Thrall's people in the hope of stopping the bloodshed.

As for Arthas, he had become one of the greatest

evils in the world. Now Jaina found herself in a place where she trusted the leader of the orc clans more than the man she once loved or her father.

When her father had attacked, Thrall—who had seen the pain in Jaina's eyes when she told him how to defeat the admiral—had kept his word. And he had never been one to accept that the world was the way it was. He had been captured as an infant and raised by a human named Aedelas Blackmoore to be the perfect slave, even given a name representing that. But Thrall threw off his chains and rallied the orcs first to freedom, then to the ways of his people that had been lost to the demonic hordes that had brought them to this world.

Now, Jaina saw a different look in Thrall's unusual blue eyes. Her dear friend was furious.

"We signed no treaty, you and I." Thrall started in immediately, not even returning Jaina's greeting. "We made no provisions for our alliance. We trusted that our bond had been forged in blood, and we would never betray each other."

"I have not betrayed you, Thrall." Jaina tensed briefly, but with the ease of long practice, kept her emotions in check. She didn't appreciate the blanket accusation of betrayal without even the conversational niceties—or even an acknowledgment of their bond beyond his out-of-nowhere belief that she'd broken it—but the first thing she had been taught as an apprentice mage was that strong emotions and wizardry didn't always mix well. She increased her grip on the ornate wooden staff she carried, a legacy from her mentor, Archmage Antonidas.

"I do not believe *you* have." Thrall's tone was still belligerent. Unlike his fellow orcs, gruffness was not Thrall's default manner, no doubt due to his human upbringing. "However, it seems your people may not hold to our bond as strongly as you."

Her voice tight, Jaina asked, "Thrall, what are you talking about?"

"One of our merchant vessels, the *Orgath'ar*, was harassed by pirates."

Jaina frowned. As much as they tried to prevent it, privateering remained a problem on the seas. "We've increased the patrols as much as possible, but—"

"Patrols are useless if they are just going to sit and watch! The *Orgath'ar* saw one of your patrols nearby! It was close enough to be seen in dense fog, yet they did *nothing* to aid Captain Bolik and his crew! Bolik even sounded the foghorn, and your people just *sat.*"

Her calm in inverse proportion to Thrall's anger, Jaina asked, "You say your lookout could see them. That doesn't necessarily mean that they could see *Orgath'ar.*"

That brought Thrall up short.

Jaina continued. "Your people have better vision than we do. And when they heard the foghorn, they probably took it as a sign to get out of the way."

"If they were close enough for my people to see, they were close enough to *hear* a boarding party! My people have better vision, it's true, but we also do not do battle in stealth. I do *not* believe that your patrol did not *hear* what happened."

"Thrall—"

The orc turned around, throwing his hands into the air. "I had thought that things would be different here! I had thought that your people had finally come to accept mine as equals. I should have realized that when it came to taking up arms against their own to aid an orc, humans would abandon us."

Now Jaina was having a harder time reining in her temper. "How dare you? *I* had thought that, after all we'd been through, you'd at least give my people the benefit of the doubt."

"The evidence—"

"What evidence? To whom have you spoken besides this Captain Bolik and his crew?"

Thrall's silence answered Jaina's question.

"I will find out which patrol ship it was. Where was *Orgath'ar* attacked?"

"Half a league off the coast near Ratchet, an hour from port."

Jaina nodded. "I'll have one of my soldiers investigate. Those patrols are coordinated by Northwatch."

Thrall tensed.

"What is it?"

The orc turned back around to face her. "There is considerable pressure on me to take Northwatch Keep back by force."

"And there is considerable pressure on me to keep it."

Thrall and Jaina stared at each other. Now that he faced her again, Jaina saw something different in the orc's blue eyes: not anger, but confusion.

"How did this happen?" Thrall asked the question in a quieter voice, all belligerence now seemingly burned out of him. "How did it come to where we bicker over such idiocy?"

Jaina couldn't help but laugh. "We are leaders, Thrall."

"Leaders take their warriors into battle."

"In times of war, yes," Jaina said. "In times of peace, they lead them differently. War is a grand endeavor that subsumes daily existence, but when it ends, there is still daily existence." She walked over to her old comrade and put her small hand on his massive arm. "I will investigate this, Thrall, and learn the truth. And if my soldiers did not do their duty by our alliance, then I swear to you they *will* be punished."

Thrall nodded. "Thank you, Jaina. And I apologize for my accusations. But my people have endured so much. *I* have endured so much, and I will not see our people mistreated again."

"Nor will I," Jaina said quietly. "And perhaps—" She hesitated.

"What?"

"Perhaps we *should* draft a formal treaty. Because you were right before—you and I may trust each other, but not all humans and orcs will do likewise. And much as we may wish it otherwise, we will not live forever."

Thrall nodded. "It is often . . . difficult to remind my people that you are no longer our slavemasters. In many ways, they wish to continue the rebellion even though the time of orc enslavement is long past. Sometimes I get caught up in their fervor, especially since I was raised in bondage by a creature as foul as any member of the Burning Legion. Sometimes I believe the worst, and so will my people when I am gone and can no longer remind them. So perhaps you are correct."

"Let us solve this crisis first," Jaina said, giving Thrall a smile. "Then we will speak of treaties."

"Thank you." Then Thrall shook his head and chuckled.

"What is it?"

"You are nothing like her in any way, but—when you smiled, just for an instant, you reminded me of Tari."

Jaina remembered that Taretha Foxton, whom most called Tari, was the daughter of a member of Aedelas Blackmoore's household, and had been instrumental in Thrall's escape from Blackmoore's clutches at the cost of her own life.

Orcs immortalized their history in song form: a *lok'-amon* chronicled the starting of a family, a *lok'tra* a battle, a *lok'vadnod* the life of a hero. To the best of anyone's knowledge, the only human ever to have a *lok'vadnod* sung of her life was named Tari.

And so Jaina bowed her head and said, "I am honored to be so associated. I will send Colonel Lorena to North-watch, and as soon as she reports, I will inform you."

Thrall shook his head. "Another woman in your military. Humans astound me sometimes."

Jaina's tone grew frosty; again, she tightly gripped the staff. "What do you mean? Can men and women not be equals in your world?"

"Of course not. Nor would I say," he added quickly before Jaina could interrupt, "that they are unequal—any more than I would say that an insect and a flower could be equals. They serve completely different purposes."

Grateful for the opening, Jaina said the same thing to Thrall that she had said to Antonidas when as a brash young woman she had insisted on becoming his apprentice. Back then, the archmage had said to her, "It is no more women's nature to become wizards than it is a dog's nature to compose an aria."

As then, she now said to Thrall: "Is not what separates us from animals that we can change our nature? After all, there are those who would argue that an orc's nature was to be a slave." Then Jaina shook her head. "However, there are many who think as you do. It is why women have to work twice as hard to achieve the same position as a man—which is why I trust Lorena more than any of my other colonels. She will learn the truth."

At that, Thrall threw his massive head back and laughed heartily. "You are a fine woman, Jaina Proudmoore. You remind me how much I still have to learn about humans, despite having been raised by them."

"Given who raised you, I'd say that was more *because* you were raised by them."

Thrall nodded. "A fine point. Have your female colonel investigate the matter. We will speak again when she is done." He moved toward the rope ladder that still dangled from the hovering airship.

"Thrall." He stopped and turned to face her. She gave him as encouraging a look as she could. "We will not let this alliance fail."

Again, he nodded. "No, we shall not." With that, he climbed the rope.

Jaina, for her part, muttered an incantation in a language known only to mages, then took a deep breath. Her stomach felt as if it were being sucked out through her nose, as the butte, the airship, Thrall, and Razor Hill shifted and altered around her, growing indistinct and hazy. A moment, and then everything coalesced into the familiar surroundings of her chambers on the top floor of the largest of the castles that made up the tallest structures in Theramore.

She did most of the work of state here, in this small room with its desk and thousands of scrolls, rather than in the throne room, an ostentatious title for a like space. Jaina sat in that throne as little as possible—even during the weekly occasions when she saw petitioners, she generally paced in front of the embarrassingly large chair rather than actually park herself in it—and used the room sparingly. These chambers felt more like Antonidas's study, where she learned her craft, complete with disorganized desk and badly sorted scrolls. That made it feel like home.

Something else the throne room had that the chambers didn't was a window with a view. Jaina knew she'd never get any work done if there was a view of Theramore—she would be distracted alternately by wonder at what they'd built here and fright at her responsibility for it.

Teleporting was always an intense, draining process, and while Jaina's training allowed her to be battle-ready instantly upon completing a teleport, all things being equal, she preferred to give herself a little time to recover. She gave herself those moments now before calling out to her secretary. "Duree!"

The old widow came in through the main entrance. The chambers had three entrances. Two of them were known to all: the one Duree had just used, and the one to the hallway and staircase that led to Jaina's private apartments. The third was a secret passageway meant to be an escape route. Only six other people knew of it, and five of those were the workers who had built it.

Duree glared at Jaina through her spectacles. "No need to shout, I'm sitting right outside the door like I always am. How'd your meeting with the orc go?"

Sighing, Jaina said, not for the first time, "His name is *Thrall.*"

Duree waved her arms about so much that the frail woman almost lost her balance. Her spectacles fell off her nose and dangled from their string around her neck. "I know, but it's such a stupid name. I mean, orcs have names like Hellscream and Doomhammer and Drek'Than and Burx and the like, and he calls himself *Thrall*? What self-respecting orc would call himself that?"

Not bothering to explain that Thrall was more self-respecting than any orc she'd known—since the explanation had never worked the previous hundred times she'd tried it—Jaina said instead, "It's Drek'Thar, not Drek'Than."

"Either way." Duree put her spectacles back on her nose. "Those are good orc names. Not Thrall. Anyhow, how'd it go?"

"We have a problem. Get Kristoff in here, and have one of the boys find Colonel Lorena and tell her to put a detail together that's traveling to Northwatch, and then to report to me." Jaina sat at her desk and started sorting through the scrolls, trying to find the shipping reports.

"Why Lorena? Shouldn't you get Lothar or Pierce? Someone less—I don't know, *feminine*? They're a rough bunch in Northwatch."

Wondering if she was going to have this conversation every time Lorena's name came up, Jaina said, "Lorena's tougher than Lothar and Pierce combined. She'll be fine."

Duree pouted, a poor sight on such an old woman. "It ain't right. Military ain't women's work."

Giving up on finding the shipping records, she instead glared at her secretary. "Neither is running a city-state."

"Well, that's different," Duree said weakly.

"How?"

"It just *is*."

Jaina shook her head. Three years, and Duree had yet to come up with a better answer than that. "Just go get Kristoff and send for Lorena before I turn you into a newt."

"You turn me into a newt, you'll never find anything again."

Throwing up her hands in frustration. "I can't find anything *now*. Where *are* the damn shipping records?"

Smiling, Duree said, "Kristoff has 'em. I'll tell him to bring 'em when he comes, shall I?"

"Please."

Duree bowed, which caused her spectacles to fall off again. Then she left the chambers. Jaina briefly considered throwing a fireball after her, but decided against it. Duree was right—without her, Jaina never would be able to find anything.

Moments later, Kristoff arrived, several scrolls in hand. "Duree said you wanted to see me, milady. Or did you just want these?" He indicated the scrolls.

"Both, actually. Thank you," she added as she took the scrolls from him.

Kristoff was Jaina's chamberlain. While she ruled Theramore, Kristoff was the one who *ran* it. His capacity for irritating minutiae made him ideal for the job, and had been the primary thing keeping Jaina from indulging in a homicidal rage when being leader became too much for her not-very-broad shoulders to bear. He had been the clerk to Highlord Garithos before the war, when his organizational skills had become legendary.

Certainly, he did not advance in the military due to any physical prowess. Kristoff was tall but rail thin, seeming almost as fragile as Duree, who at least had old age to blame. His straight, dark, just-past-shoulder-length hair framed an angular face and hawk nose, a visage that seemed to wear a perpetual scowl.

Jaina shared Thrall's story of the attack on *Orgath'ar* and the nearby vessel doing nothing to help.

Raising a thin eyebrow, Kristoff said, "The story does not seem credible. Half a league off Ratchet, you said?"

Jaina nodded.

"There were no military boats assigned to that region, milady."

"The fog was thick—it's possible that the boat Captain Bolik saw was off course."

Kristoff nodded, conceding the point. "However, milady, it is also possible that Captain Bolik was mistaken."

"It seems unlikely." Jaina walked around to the other side of her desk and sat in the chair, placing the shipping records on the only open space. "Orcs have keener eyesight than we do, remember, and they tend to use the most gifted in eyesight as lookouts."

"We must also consider the possibility that the orcs are lying." Before Jaina could object to this notion—

which she very much intended to do—Kristoff held up a long-fingered hand. "I do not speak of Thrall, now, milady. The orcs' Warchief is an honorable man, it's true. You do well to place your trust in him, and I believe that he is simply relaying what he was told by his people."

"Then what are you saying?" Jaina knew the answer to the question, but wanted to hear Kristoff confirm it.

"I am saying the same thing that I have said to you all along, milady—we cannot afford to blindly trust the orcs. Individual orcs have proven honorable, yes, but orcs as a whole? We would be fools to assume that they all wish us well, and that they all will be as enlightened as Thrall. He was a strong ally against the Burning Legion, and I have nothing but admiration for what he has done—but what he has done is temporary." Kristoff set his thin hands down on the desk, leaning toward Jaina. "The only thing keeping the orcs in line is Thrall, and the minute he is gone, I can assure you, milady, the orcs will revert to type and do everything they can to destroy us."

Jaina barked a laugh, involuntarily. Kristoff's words mirrored Jaina and Thrall's conversation—yet it seemed less rational coming out of the chamberlain's mouth.

Kristoff straightened. "Something amuses you, milady?"

"No. I believe you are overestimating the situation."

"And I believe you are underestimating it. This city-state is all that keeps Kalimdor from being run entirely by the orcs." Kristoff hesitated, which was unusual. The chamberlain had made a career out of being forthright, which was one of his more useful characteristics.

"What is it, Kristoff?"

"Our allies are . . . concerned. The notion of an entire continent under orc rule is . . . disturbing to many. At present, little is being done, in part because there are other issues, but—"

"But right now I'm all that is preventing an invasion?"

"As long as the Lady Proudmoore—great wizard, victor against the Burning Legion—rules the humans on Kalimdor, the rest of the world will sleep well at night. The moment they believe that the Lady Proudmoore cannot keep the orcs in line, that will change. And the invasion force will make your late father's fleet look like a pair of rowboats."

Jaina leaned back in her chair. In truth, she had given little thought to the world beyond Kalimdor, busy as she had been with fighting the demons and then building Theramore. And her own father's attack drove home the fact that those who had not actually fought alongside the orcs still viewed them as little more than animals.

But Kristoff should have known better. "What is it you are suggesting, Chamberlain?"

"That this Captain Bolik might be an agitator, trying to turn Thrall against you—against *us*. Even with Northwatch, we are very much alone within Theramore's gates, and could easily find ourselves surrounded by orcs—and more, with the trolls already on their side and the goblins unlikely to take any side."

Jaina shook her head. Kristoff's prediction was the worst nightmare of every human living on Kalimdor. It seemed like only yesterday that they were well on the road to making those nightmares an impossibility. Trade with the orcs was going smoothly, the Barrens— neutral territory between Durotar and Theramore— had been peaceful and orderly, and the two species that had once despised each other had lived in peace for three years.

The question Jaina now asked herself was whether or not this was a portent of how things should be, or simply a resting period while they recovered from the Burning Legion and just the calm before the inevitable storm?

Before Jaina could contemplate further, a tall, dark-haired woman with a square face, pointed nose, and broad shoulders entered. She wore the standard military uniform of plate armor with a green tabbard depicting the anchor-shaped emblem of Kul Tiras, the former home of the Proudmoore family.

Raising her right hand to her forehead in salute, she said, "Colonel Lorena reporting as ordered, milady."

Standing, Jaina said, "Thank you, Colonel. Stand easy. Duree told you what is required?" Jaina always felt short next to Lorena and so preferred to stand in her presence, to give herself as much height as her smaller form would provide.

Lowering her hand and putting both arms behind

her back, but otherwise still standing ramrod straight with perfect posture, Lorena said, "Yes, ma'am, she did. We leave for Northwatch within the hour, and I've sent a runner to inform Major Davin of our arrival."

"Good. That'll be all, both of you."

Lorena saluted, turned on her heel, and exited. Kristoff, however, hung back a moment.

When the chamberlain refused to speak, Jaina prompted him. "What is it, Kristoff?"

"It might be wise to have the detail accompanying Lorena remain at Northwatch to fortify it."

Without hesitation, Jaina said, "No."

"Milady—"

"The orcs want us out of Northwatch altogether, Kristoff. And while I understand why we can't accede to that request, I am *not* going to do something as provocative as reinforce it, especially when they believe that we refused to help them against pirates."

"I still think—"

"You've been excused, Chamberlain," Jaina said frostily.

Kristoff glowered at her for a moment before bowing low, spreading his arms, and saying, "Milady," before taking his leave.

FOUR

I'm not sure I understand what the problem is, Colonel."

Lorena stared out the window of the small watch office for Northwatch Keep. The statement had been made by Major Davin, the current commandant of Northwatch, who had been frustrating Lorena since she and her six-soldier detail arrived an hour ago.

From his seat at the small desk in the watch office's center, Davin, a stout man with a thick beard, had told Lorena that there was a convoy ship that had gotten lost in the fog. It was possible that that was the ship the orcs claimed to have seen.

Lorena turned to look down at him—made easy by his being seated, though Lorena was taller than the major even when standing—and said, "The problem, Major, is that the orcs were expecting help from us. And they should've gotten it."

"What for?" Davin sounded genuinely confused.

"They're our *allies.*" Lorena couldn't believe she needed to explain this. Davin was a hero during the war, having been the only survivor of a brutal massacre of his platoon, which was escorting a wizard who was also killed. The intelligence he brought back had been invaluable.

But now the war hero just shrugged. "They fought with us, sure, but that was necessity. Colonel, they're not even *civilized.* Only reason to put up with 'em's 'cause of Thrall, and he's only worth it 'cause he was raised by humans. But what happens to them ain't our concern."

"Lady Proudmoore disagrees with that sentiment," Lorena said in a tight voice, "and so do I." She turned back around. The view of the Great Sea from this window was quite spectacular, and Lorena found she preferred it to looking at Davin's annoying face. "I've sent my people to find Captain Avinal and his crew to get their side of the story."

Now Davin stood up. "With all due respect, Colonel, there's no 'side.' Avinal's boat got lost. They got back on course. They came home. If an orc ship got itself attacked by pirates, then fine, but it's not our problem."

"Yes, actually, it is." She refused to turn to look at him. "Pirates, on the whole, aren't especially picky about who they attack. They'll go after goblins, orcs, trolls, ogres, elves, dwarves—or humans. If there *are* pirates operating that close to Ratchet, it *does* concern us."

"I've been assigned to this post for three years,

Colonel." Davin sounded petulant now. "I don't need you to tell me about pirates."

"If that's the case, then you shouldn't need me to remind you why an orc ship being harassed is your concern."

A small private whose uniform looked as if it had been fitted for someone a full head taller, knocked meekly on the door to the watch office. "Uh, sir, there's some people here to see you and Colonel Lorena, sir, if that's okay, sir."

"Who?" Davin asked.

"Uh, Captain Avinal, sir, and a soldier I don't know, sir."

"That'd be Strov," Lorena said. "He's the one I told to bring the captain here."

Davin fixed Lorena with a glare. "And what's the use of embarrassing the man by bringin' him up to the watch office like a common prisoner?"

Lorena started mentally composing the letter to Lady Proudmoore and General Norris recommending that Davin be reassigned to kitchen detail. "First of all, Major, I would think you'd prefer that I talk to your captain in your presence. Secondly—do you usually bring criminals to the watch office rather than the brig?"

Apparently, Davin was content to continue glaring rather than answer her question.

So Lorena turned to the young officer. "Send them both in please, Private."

Irritatingly, the private looked to Davin first. The

major nodded, and only then did the private go back out.

Two men then entered the small office. Strov was the most average person Lorena knew—average height, weight, and build, brown hair, brown eyes, small mustache. He looked like every other adult human male in the world, which was one of several reasons why he was such a good tracker. So nondescript was he that nobody noticed he was there.

Following Strov was a man with the weathered look of an experienced sailor. His gait was awkward, as if he walked expecting the deck to buckle under him, and his face bore the wrinkles and redness of long exposure to the sun.

"Captain Avinal," Davin said, moving back to his chair, "this is Colonel Lorena. Lady Proudmoore sent her up from Theramore to find out why a pirate ship attacked an orc ship."

Avinal frowned. "I'd think that'd be obvious, Colonel."

Sparing a moment to give Davin a glare of her own, Lorena then regarded Avinal. "The major's stated reason for my being here is not quite accurate. I know why a pirate ship attacked an orc trader—what I don't know is why you didn't help them."

Pointing at Strov, Avinal asked, "That why this man and his people've been harassin' my crew?"

"Private Strov and his comrades are following the lady's orders, Captain, as am I."

"I've got a patrol to make, ma'am. There any way this can wait—"

"No, Captain, there isn't."

Avinal looked at Davin. Davin shrugged, as if to say that it was out of his hands. Then the captain looked witheringly at Lorena. "Fine. When's this attack supposed to've happened?"

"Five days ago. According to Major Davin you were fogbound that morning."

"Yes'm, we were."

"Did you see any other ships that morning?"

"Might've—some shapes that might'a been a boat here an' there, but couldn't be sure. We were near a boat at one point, I know that much—rang their foghorn."

Lorena nodded. That tracked with what the orcs told Lady Proudmoore.

"But we didn't see nothin' solid. Couldn't see the nose in front of your face, and that's a fact. Fifty years, I been sailin', Colonel, and I ain't never seen fog the like of that. Sargeras himself could've taken a stroll on the deck and I might not'a seen it. It was all I could do to keep my own people from mutiny, truth be told. Last thing any of us'd be concerned about is a buncha greenskins."

For several seconds, Lorena stared at the captain. Then she sighed. "Very well, Captain, thank you. That will be all."

Muttering, "Blessed waste of time," under his breath, Avinal departed.

After the captain left, Strov said, "Most of the crew say the same, ma'am."

"Of course they do," Davin said. "Because it's the truth, as'd be obvious to anyone who'd think about it for a second."

Whirling on the major, Lorena asked, "Tell me, Major, why didn't you mention that Captain Avinal was near another boat—or that it rang its foghorn?"

"I didn't think it was relevant."

Lorena changed her mental letter so that Davin would be transferred to cesspool duty. "It isn't your job to assess relevance, Major. It's your job—your duty—to follow the orders of your superiors."

Davin let out a long breath. "Look, Colonel—you were sent here to find out if Captain Avinal did anything wrong. He didn't. And what does it matter if a bunch of greenskins got their cargo took?"

"Actually, they didn't—they fought off the pirates on their own."

Now Davin stood again, looking at Lorena like she was mad. "Then—with all due respect, ma'am, what's the meaning of this inquiry? It's not like the greenskins *needed* our help—so why treat us like criminals? As I said, we did nothing wrong."

Lorena shook her head, not agreeing with that statement at all.

FIVE

Byrok never imagined that the happiest time in his life would be when he went fishing.

On the face of it, it didn't seem to be the life for an orc. Fishing involved no battle, no glory, no challenging combat, no testing of one's mettle against an equal foe. No weaponry was involved, no blood was shed.

But it was less what he did than why he did it. Byrok went fishing because he was free.

As a youth, he had heard the false promises of Gul'-dan and his Shadow Council who promised a new world where the sky was blue and the inhabitants easy prey for superior orc might to conquer. Byrok, along with the others of his clan, followed Gul'dan's instructions, never knowing that he and his council did the bidding of Sargeras and his foul demons, never realizing that the price for this new world would be their very souls.

It took a decade for the orcs to be defeated. Either they were enslaved by the demons they thought were their benefactors, or they were enslaved by the humans, who proved to have more fight in them than the demons imagined.

Demon magic had made Byrok's memories of his life in the orcs' native land dim. A lack of interest in remembering had had a similar effect on his recollections of his life in human bondage. He recalled mainly that the work was backbreaking and menial, and it destroyed what little of his spirit the demons had left intact.

Then Thrall came.

Everything changed then. The son of the great Durotan—whose death had, in many ways, been the end of the orcs' former way of life—Thrall had escaped his overseers and used the humans' own tactics against them. He reminded the orcs of their long-forgotten past.

On the day that Thrall and his growing army liberated Byrok, he swore that he would serve the young orc until one of them died.

So far, that death had not come, despite the finest efforts of human soldiers or demon hordes. One lesser member of the Burning Legion did, however, claim Byrok's right eye. In exchange, Byrok removed the demon's entire head.

When the fighting ended, and when the orcs settled in Durotar, Byrok requested that he be relieved of his service. Should the call to battle be sounded, Byrok promised he would be the first in line to take up the mantle of the warrior once again, even with one eye missing, but now he wished to make use of the freedom he had fought so hard for.

Thrall naturally granted it to him, and to all those who requested it.

Byrok did not need to fish, of course. Durotar included some excellent farmland. Since the human lands were located in the marshy territory to the south, humans could not grow crops, and so turned most of their energy to fishing. They would trade their surplus to the orcs in exchange for their surplus crops.

But Byrok wanted no fish caught by humans. He wanted nothing to do with humans if he could possibly avoid it. Yes, the humans had fought at the orcs' side against the Burning Legion, but that was an alliance of necessity. Humans were monsters, and Byrok wanted nothing to do with such uncivilized creatures.

So it was rather a shock to the one-eyed orc to find six humans in his usual fishing spot on Deadeye Shore.

For starters, the area surrounding Byrok's fishing hole was high grassland. Byrok's tracking skills had been reduced a bit by the lack of a good right eye, but he still saw no indication that any but he had traversed through the grasses—especially not any humans, who, for such small, lightweight creatures, were pathetically overt in their movements. Nor did Byrok see any airships nearby, nor any boats on the water within sight of the fishing spot.

How they arrived, though, was of considerably less concern to Byrok than the fact that they *had* arrived. Setting down his fishing gear, he unstrapped the morningstar from his back. The weapon had been a gift from Thrall after the Warchief had freed him from bondage, and Byrok went nowhere without it.

Were these fellow orcs in Byrok's spot, he would have questioned their presence, but humans—particularly human trespassers—deserved no such consideration. He would find out their intent by stealthier means. At best, they might simply be fools who strayed too far north and did not realize they were invading. Byrok had lived a long time, and had come to understand that stupidity was a far more common explanation than malice.

But at worst, these might be true invaders, and if they were, Byrok would not let them walk out of his fishing hole alive.

Byrok had learned the human language during his time in captivity, and so was able to understand the words of these six—at least those he could hear. From where he was crouched down amid the tall grass, he could hear only a few words.

The words he did hear, however, were not encouraging. "Overthrow" was one, "Thrall" another. So was "greenskin," a derogatory human term for orcs.

Then he caught the phrase, "We'll kill them all and take this continent for ourselves."

Another asked a question, the only word of which

Byrok caught was "troll." The one who wished to take the continent then said, "We'll kill them, too."

Pushing aside the grass, Byrok looked more closely at the humans. He didn't notice anything particularly distinguishing about them—all humans looked alike to Byrok—but the old orc did notice that the two closest to him had the image of a burning sword on their person: one as a tattoo on his arm, the other as an earring.

His blood running cold, Byrok remembered where he'd seen that symbol before. It was long ago, when the orcs first came to this world at Gul'dan's urging: they called themselves the Burning Blade, and their armor and flags carried the same symbol that these two humans wore. The Burning Blade were among the fiercest devotees of the Shadow Council. They were later wiped out, and none of that demon-loving clan remained.

Yet here were *humans* wearing their symbol, and speaking of killing Thrall.

His blood boiling, Byrok got to his feet and started running toward the sextet, twirling the morningstar over his head. Even with his bulk, the only noise he made as he approached was the whizzing sound of the morningstar's chain as it pivoted on the handle in Byrok's fingers and rotated along with the large spiked ball on the other end around the orc's head.

That was, unfortunately, enough. Two of the humans—the two with the Burning Blade symbol—whirled around. So Byrok targeted the nearest of those two first, throwing the morningstar right at his shaved head. He wasn't concerned about losing his weapon—no human could lift the thing, so it would be safe until he could grab it again.

"An orc!"

" 'Bout time one showed up!"

"Kill it!"

Since the element of surprise was gone, he let out a huge roar—that always intimidated humans—and leapt at another, this one with a full beard. Byrok's massive fist collided with the bearded one's head.

The one with the shaved head clutched his shoulder—he had managed to avoid being hit in the head, to Byrok's disappointment—and tried to lift the morningstar with his other hand. Had he time, Byrok would have laughed.

However, he was too busy grabbing another human's head in his right hand and preparing to throw the invader into one of his comrades. That did not happen, however, as another human attacked from the right.

Cursing himself for forgetting to account for the fact that he was now blind on that side, Byrok flailed out with his right arm, even as pain sliced into his side.

Two more humans piled on top of him, one punching him, the other going at him with a blade. Byrok managed to step on one attacker's leg, breaking it instantly. The screams of his victim served to goad the orc, and he redoubled his attack. But there were simply too many of them. Even though two of them were badly injured, they continued to pile on him, and even Byrok could not defeat six humans while unarmed.

Realizing that he needed his weapon, he inhaled deeply and then let out a huge roar even as he punched both fists outward with all his strength. It only knocked his foes off him for an instant, but an instant was all he needed. He dove for his weapon, his fingers closing around the handle.

Before he could lift it, however, two of the humans pounded on his head, and another drove a dagger through his left thigh. Byrok flailed his arm outward, the morningstar's ball sailing through the air, just missing the humans.

Then, much as he loathed himself for being forced to do it, Byrok ran.

It was a hard thing for him, and not just because the dagger that was still protruding from his thigh slowed his gait. To run from battle was shameful. But Byrok knew he had a higher duty to perform—the Burning Blade had returned, only this time they were humans. And *all* the attackers, not just the two he'd noticed before, wore that flaming sword image somewhere on them: a necklace, a tattoo, *something*.

This was information that needed to get back to Thrall.

So Byrok ran.

Or, rather, he hobbled. His wounds were taking their toll. It became a struggle even to breathe.

But still he ran.

Dimly, he registered that the six humans were giving chase, but he couldn't afford to pay attention to that. He had to get back to Orgrimmar and tell Thrall what was happening. Even with his injury, his strides were greater than those of the humans, and he could outrun them. Once he pulled far enough ahead, he would lose them in the underbrush of this land that he knew better than any outsider possibly could. Besides, they only seemed to want to beat up an orc. They probably did not realize that Byrok understood their gutter tongue, and therefore they did not know that Byrok knew who they were. They would not chase him past the point where it would be useful to them.

Or so he hoped.

No longer were there any thoughts in Byrok's mind. He cleared his head of all save the critical imperative of putting one foot down in front of the other, the ground slamming into his soles. He ignored the pain in his leg, and in all the other places they'd beat or cut him, ignored the fact that his one good eye was getting foggy, ignored the fatigue that drained the strength from his limbs.

Still he ran.

Then he stumbled. His left leg refused to lift as it was supposed to—but his right leg continued to run, and so he crashed to the ground, high grass and dirt getting in his nose and mouth and eye.

"Must . . . get . . . up . . ."

"You ain't goin' nowhere, monster." Byrok could

hear the voice, hear the humans' footfalls, and then feel the pressure when two of them sat on his back, immobilizing him. " 'Cause, here's the thing—your time is over. Orcs don't belong in this world, and so we're gonna take you out of it. Got me?"

Byrok managed the effort of lifting his head so he could see two of the humans. He spat at them.

The humans just laughed. "Let's do it, boys. *Galtak Ered'nash!*"

The other five all replied in kind: "*Galtak Ered'nash!*" Then they started beating the orc.

SIX

An hour after she had finished questioning Davin and Avinal, Colonel Lorena gathered her detail at a clearing just outside Northwatch. Rocks and thick trees dotted the landscape, and sagebrush poked out through the uneven ground. The sun shone down on the ground and the flora, making everything seem to glow—and also keeping everyone quite warm in their plate mail.

Most of the detail Lorena took were simply the top names on the duty roster, but she had hand-picked two of them. Though young, Strov was her most trusted soldier—he did his duty without question, could improvise when necessary, but when it wasn't, would follow orders to the letter. He could also follow anyone without losing them or letting his prey know he was there.

The other was the opposite of Strov: Jalod was an old soldier who had fought against orcs back when nobody knew what an orc was. Rumor had it that he had trained

Admiral Proudmoore, though Lorena put very little stock in that one. Either way, he'd seen everything, done everything, and lived to tell exaggerated stories about all of it.

Strov said, "Like I said in the watch office, ma'am, the other crew corroborated what Captain Avinal said. They couldn't see a thing out there. I doubt they had any confirmation that either *Orgath'ar* or the pirates were even there."

"And if they were," another soldier, a veteran named Paolo, added, "they weren't in no shape to be helpin' nobody. Sailors I talked to was scared when they spoke of it."

Mal, who'd served in Azeroth's navy years ago, nodded. "Can't blame 'em. Fog's the worst. No way to get your bearings. Usually best to just drop anchor till it passes. Surprised they didn't, truth be told."

"What does it matter?"

That was Jalod. Lorena frowned. "What do you—?"

"Them orcs decimated Admiral Proudmoore's fleet! Killed one of the finest men ever to draw breath! If it were me in charge of Avinal's boat, I'd'a been helpin' the pirates. It's shameful is what it is, Lady Proudmoore betraying her own to those savages—betraying her own *father* for such as they. It's shameful that she's got us doing this when we should be goin' after those monsters!"

Everyone shifted uncomfortably on their feet at those words.

That is, everyone except for Lorena, who unsheathed

her sword and put the point right at Jalod's throat. The old man seemed surprised at that, and his blue eyes grew wide with fear, even under the folds of wrinkly flesh that covered his face.

Speaking in a low and dangerous tone, Lorena said, "Never speak ill of Lady Proudmoore in my presence again, Sergeant. I don't care who you served with or how many trolls and demons you've killed, if you *ever* even *think* such thoughts about Lady Proudmoore, I will tear you open stem to stern and feed the pieces to the dogs. Do I make myself clear?"

Strov stepped forward. "I'm sure the sergeant meant no disrespect to Lady Proudmoore, ma'am."

"Course not." Jalod's voice was shakier now. "I ain't got nothin' but respect for her, ma'am, you know that. It's just—"

"Just *what*?"

Jalod swallowed, his Adam's apple butting up against Lorena's sword point. "Them orcs can't be trusted is all I'm sayin'."

That *wasn't* all Jalod was saying, but Lorena lowered her sword anyhow. Jalod's decades of service earned him the benefit of several dozen doubts, and those words were very much out of character for a man who had eagerly served under Lady Proudmoore for years now, going back to the days before Arthas turned. Indeed, had it been anyone else, she would not have bothered with the warning and would have gone straight to the disemboweling.

Sheathing her sword, Lorena said, "Let's head back to the dock. We've got a long trip home."

As they marched back toward the docks where their transport ship was berthed, Lorena wondered what was going on. She'd been a soldier for all of her adult life. The youngest of ten children, and the only girl, she'd wanted to be a soldier just like her brothers and father. She had even convinced herself that she was a boy, right up until she reached her thirteenth summer and her body forced her to confront the reality that she was female. She was so skilled with a sword and shield that her father overcame his reluctance and sponsored her application to join the Kul Tiras City Guard. Over the years, she worked her way up the ranks, finally being promoted to colonel by Lady Proudmoore herself during the war against the Burning Legion.

Over those years she had honed her instincts—the instincts of a soldier from a family of soldiers—and those instincts now told her that there was more to this than a military convoy not seeing a trading ship or the pirates attacking them in the fog. The suspicion had been in the back of her mind from the moment she arrived at Northwatch, but Jalod's words put it to the front.

She wasn't sure what was wrong, precisely, but she intended to find out.

As they marched toward the edge of the clearing, Private Strov made sure to keep Sergeant Jalod in his sight at all times. He wasn't sure what had gotten into the old buzzard, but Strov didn't like it, not one bit.

It was one thing to complain about the orcs. That was to be expected, given the history, though Strov himself generally thought of the orcs as victims of demonic influence. Made as much sense to hate them as it did Medivh, and he was revered as a hero despite what the demons did to him. Still and all, he could see why some might view the orcs with animosity.

But Lady Proudmoore? The only ones who had reason to think ill of her were the Burning Legion and those that were sympathetic to their cause.

Jalod was never one to express such feelings in the past. Which led Strov to think that perhaps the sergeant was losing his marbles. Nothing wrong with that—it happened to the best of people—but it could endanger them. One of the things they drilled into you in training was that you had to rely on the people in your unit. Strov wasn't sure he could rely on Jalod anymore.

So intent was he on keeping the sergeant in his sight line at all times, Strov was slow to pick up on something he should have noticed earlier. The trees and rocks, along with some storage sheds used for Northwatch, provided an almost circular border. As they neared the circle's edge, Strov saw four figures in cloaks hiding behind the storage sheds, the trees, or the rocks. They were well concealed, but Strov had a keener eye than most.

"Ambush!"

At Strov's cry, all seven of them got into a fighter's crouch and unsheathed their swords. Simultaneously, seven figures—Strov had missed three of them—leapt out from cover.

The figures were massive, their cloaks doing an inadequate job of hiding the fact that they were orcs, though doing a fine job of hiding any distinguishing features they might have had.

Strov noticed something else as he parried the club that was swinging toward his head: the cloaks had an emblem on the breast of a sword on fire. That was familiar to Strov, but he couldn't take the time to follow up on the thought just at the moment, as the becloaked orc was doing everything possible to end Strov's life.

The orc swung the club thrice more, and all three times Strov parried, but on the third he also stepped in and kicked the orc in the stomach. Not expecting such an attack, the orc stumbled, and Strov thrust at it with his sword. However, the orc had the wherewithal to block the thrust with its club.

Unfortunately for the orc, this put Strov on the offensive. He kept coming with different thrusts and strikes, hoping to catch the orc unawares, but his foe was well trained and had amazingly fast reflexes—and was now ready for additional kicks or punches Strov might deliver. Many humans, Strov knew, relied wholly on their weapons to fight, but Strov had always preferred to use his entire body.

Strov thrust low, hoping that the orc would parry

low enough to open up for a strike to the head. However, the orc anticipated, and only held the club with one hand, the other hand raised and protecting its face.

So Strov kicked down at the orc's leg.

The kick wasn't hard enough to break any bones, but the orc stumbled and waved both arms to keep its balance. That gave Strov the opening he needed to run the orc through the chest.

Or so he thought. The sword managed to penetrate the cloak easily enough, about halfway up the blade, but Strov felt no penetration of flesh, and when he yanked his sword out—which took more effort than expected—there was no blood on the blade.

Strov gritted his teeth, refusing to let his surprise at not scoring first blood distract him from his foe, who was now standing steady once more.

Taking a deep breath, Strov moved in and refused to let up. He swung at the orc's neck, which was blocked, then immediately went for the stomach, then the neck again, then the legs. His arms were a blur as he pushed the orc back farther and farther, giving no quarter, barely giving his foe sufficient time to even parry—and hoping that sooner or later, that parry would not come.

Suddenly, a sword blade seemingly came out of nowhere and slashed at the orc's head. The cloak was rent by the blade, and half of it fell off to reveal the angry green face of a male orc. His left tusk had that burning sword emblem engraved in it.

The blade in question belonged to Colonel Lorena.

Strov assumed that she had dispatched her own foe.

As for the orc, he yelled out the word for retreat in the orcish tongue, and then they all yelled the phrase, *"Galtak Ered'nash!"* Strov knew many languages, including those of the orcs, trolls, goblins, and dwarves, as well as all four elven dialects. He'd never heard that phrase before.

His foe now running away, Strov turned to see that Ian and Mal were down—the former dead with his throat ripped open, the latter alive but with a leg injury—but besides himself, Lorena, Jalod, Paolo, and Clai were uninjured. One of the orcs lay on the ground as well. The other six were retreating, two of them bleeding.

"Strov, Clai, give chase," Lorena said as she ran toward Mal.

Clai was the most brutal fighter in the detail. Strov noted that his fellow private had a great deal of orc blood on his sword. "You were able to strike flesh?" Strov asked as they ran in the same direction as the remaining six orcs.

Nodding, Clai said, "Only when I got the head or the neck. It's like their bodies were made outta smoke or somethin'."

The figures had all gone through one of the overhanging willow branches that almost served as a wall. Only a few paces behind, Clai and Strov ran through to find—

—nothing. Of the orcs, there was no sign. Even the blood trail of the two injured ones was gone. The ground was visible for half a league—it was impossible for the orcs to have gone from sight in the time available.

Strov stopped short and took a deep breath. "You smell that?"

Clai shook his head.

"Sulfur. And spices—thyme, I think."

Sounding confused, Clai asked, "So?"

"Magic. Which also explains why they couldn't be stabbed."

An almost manic gleam in his eye, Clai asked, "Demons?"

"Pray not." Strov shuddered. Clai was but a youth, a recent recruit who had been too young to fight the Burning Legion. His eagerness to fight demons was that of one who had never had to fight any.

Turning, Strov ran back through the leaves toward Lorena, Clai on his heels.

The colonel was kneeling by Mal, along with Paolo, the latter binding Mal's wounds. Upon seeing Strov and Clai, she got to her feet and angrily asked, "What happened?"

"They disappeared, ma'am. Completely—even their blood trail. And there's the stink of magic."

Lorena spat. "Dammit!" She let out a breath through her teeth, then pointed at the cloak on the ground. "But that figures. That one won't be questioned, it seems."

Looking closely, Strov saw that the cloak was flat on the ground. Using his sword, he poked the garment, which disturbed some ashes. Then he looked back at the colonel.

"Definitely magic," she said with a nod.

"Ma'am, something's familiar about—" Then, finally, Strov placed it, recalling a recent conversation with his brother. "That's it!"

"What's it, Private?"

"When last I was home, my brother Manuel told me of a group that calls itself the Burning Blade. Someone tried to recruit him for it the last time he was in the Demonsbane. Said they're looking for people to come to their meetings who aren't happy with the way things are, but didn't say no more than that."

Jalod snorted. "Ain't nobody happy with the way things are. Ain't no reason to be havin' meetin's about it."

Strov thought this was odd, given what Jalod had been saying earlier, but did not respond directly, instead continuing his report to the colonel. "Ma'am, the orc I fought had a sword afire carved into his tusk."

"A burning blade." Lorena shook her head. "The one I fought—the one that turned to ashes over there—had a burning blade of his own dangling from his nose ring."

Clai raised a hand. "If I may, ma'am?" Lorena nodded. "One of my foes had one—it was like the one Private Strov fought, ma'am, on his tusk."

"Dammit." She looked over at Paolo, who was now standing over Mal. "How is he?"

"Needs a real healer, but it'll keep till we get back to Theramore." He looked past Lorena toward the main part of Northwatch. "I wouldn't trust no infirmary in this place, ma'am."

Through gritted teeth, Mal said, "Second that, ma'am."

"Fine." Sheathing her sword without wiping it down—Strov assumed she'd do it once they were under way in the boat—Lorena started toward the docks. "Let's get to the ship and give him some of my whiskey to ease the pain when we board."

Smiling raggedly, Mal said, "The colonel's a generous woman."

Giving the corporal a half smile in return, Lorena said, "Not *that* generous—just two fingers, and no more. That stuff's expensive."

Paolo signaled to Clai, and the two of them picked Mal up, keeping his wounded leg steady while they carried him, each on a side, toward the docks. Strov, meanwhile, picked up Ian's bloodied corpse.

Lorena said to him as they walked, "Private, as soon as we're back in Theramore, I want you to talk to your brother. I want to know everything possible about this Burning Blade."

"Yes, ma'am."

SEVEN

The stone-walled room that housed Thrall's seat of power as Warchief of the Horde was chilly. Thrall liked it that way—orcs were not creatures of cold, so they were uncomfortable here. He found that it was best for people not to be comfortable while in the presence of their leader. So when the place was constructed, he had made sure the stonework was thick and there were no windows. Illumination was provided only by lanterns, rather than torches, since they gave off less heat.

Not that it was ever so cold as to be truly unpleasant. He did not want his people to suffer when they were petitioning him, but nor did he want them to be entirely at ease. It had been a difficult road that Thrall had traveled, and he knew how precious—and precarious—his current position was. He would therefore take advantage of every opportunity he could, even so minor a one as keeping his throne room a bit on the cold side.

He met now with Kalthar, his shaman, and Burx, his strongest warrior. Both stood before Thrall, who sat on the leather chair made from the hides of creatures Thrall himself had slain.

"The humans are still in Northwatch Keep. Last we heard, a ship with more troops was showing up. Sounds to me like they're reinforcing."

"Hardly." Thrall leaned back in his chair. "Lady Proudmoore informed me that she was sending one of her warriors to investigate Captain Bolik's report."

Burx drew himself up. "They don't trust a warrior's word?"

Kalthar, whose green skin had grown pale and wrinkled with age, laughed throatily. "I am sure, Burx, that they trust the word of an orc as much as you would trust the word of a human."

"Humans are cowardly and despicable," Burx said dismissively.

"The humans of Theramore are no such thing." Thrall leaned forward. "And I will not hear them being spoken ill of in my presence again."

Burx stamped his foot. Thrall had to restrain a laugh at the warrior's expense. The gesture reminded Thrall of a human child throwing a temper tantrum; however, among orcs, the action was a legitimate sign of displeasure. For all he was lord of the clans, there were times when Thrall had to forcibly remind himself that he had not been raised among his own kind.

"This is *our* land, Thrall! Ours! The humans don't

have *any* claim to it. Let them go back across the Great Sea where they belong and let us get back to what life was like before the demons cursed us—away from *all* foul influences, mortal or not."

Thrall shook his head. He'd thought these arguments had ended two years ago. "The humans occupy the harshest land on Kalimdor, and precious little of it. We didn't even take the Dustwallow Marshes. Jaina's people—"

" 'Jaina'?" Burx sneered the name.

Now Thrall stood. "Be very careful, Burx. Lady Proudmoore—Jaina—has earned my respect. You, on the other hand, are rapidly losing it."

Burx cowered a bit. "I'm sorry, Warchief—but you gotta understand, you were raised with them. It can sometimes—blind you to what's obvious to the rest of us."

"I am blind to *nothing*, Burx. You may recall that it was I who opened the eyes of orcs throughout this world who had fallen prey to the demonic curse and to human imprisonment, and reminded them of *who they were*. Do *not* presume to lecture me now on—"

They were interrupted by a breathless young orc who ran in. "Thunder lizards!"

Thrall blinked. Thunder Ridge, the home of the creatures in question, was far from here—if there were any in Orgrimmar, there would have been greater warning.

"Where?" Burx asked.

"Far from here, obviously," Kalthar said witheringly, "otherwise there would have been more than a young messenger."

The boy did indeed wear the lightning-shaped nose ring that indicated a messenger. No doubt he had run from Thunder Ridge to report to Thrall. "Speak," Thrall said to the youth.

"I'm from Drygulch Ravine, Warchief. The thunder lizards, they've escaped the ridge, they have."

"How's that possible?" Burx asked.

Glaring at the warrior, Thrall said, "Let him speak, and perhaps we shall learn." To the boy, he said, "Continue."

"A farmer, name of Tulk, he heard himself a stampede. He went callin' his sons to him, and they drove the lizards off, they did, afore they destroyed his crops. But nobody never heard of no thunder lizards leavin' the ridge afore, so he went gatherin' up his sons and the next farmer over and *his* sons, and they all went to the ridge, they did."

Thrall nodded. Thunder Ridge was bordered by a dense forest of thick-trunked trees that the lizards could not rampage through. One could travel gingerly or lithely through the forests, but thunder lizards were never creatures who moved thus.

"When they got there, they saw that the forest had been razed down to nothin', it had. Lizards, they got themselves a clear path outta the ridge. The farmers are fearin' for their crops, they are."

Thrall, however, was still back on the first part. "Razed? Razed how, precisely?"

"The trees, they was all cut down. Stumps left was only a handswidth or so above the ground."

Burx asked, "Where were they taken?"

The boy shrugged. "Dunno. They didn't see no branches, nothin', just the stumps."

Shaking his head, Thrall asked, "How is this possible?"

"Don't see how it *is* possible, Warchief," the boy said, "but that's what happened, sure as I'm talkin' to you."

"You've done well." Thrall saluted the boy. "Find yourself some food and drink. There may be more questions for you after you've had your fill."

Nodding, the boy said, "Thank you, Warchief," and ran out.

"The humans," Burx said as soon as the boy had left the throne room. "It's gotta be. They've asked for wood from the trees in Thunder Ridge lots of times. Certainly no orc would defile the land like that."

Although Thrall was reluctant to believe ill of the humans, Burx was right that no orc of Durotar would do such a thing. "They could not have transported so much lumber from Thunder Ridge to the coast without anyone noticing. If they went by land, they'd be seen— same if they went by airship."

"There is a third way," Kalthar said.

Sighing, Thrall shook his head again. "Magic."

"Yes, magic," Burx said. "And the most powerful wizard in Theramore is your precious Lady Proudmoore—Jaina herself."

"It is not Lady Proudmoore," Kalthar said. "This defiling of the land is reprehensible—and the humans are both responsible, and not responsible."

"What's *that* supposed to mean?" Burx asked angrily.

"You speak in riddles," Thrall said. Then he laughed. "As usual."

"There are great forces at work here, Thrall," Kalthar said. "Powerful sorcery."

Burx stomped his foot again. "Lady Proudmoore has powerful sorcery. The humans got every reason to want those trees. It gives them stronger wood for their boats—which makes it easier for them to harass our trading ships. Plus, it lets the thunder lizards loose, which messes up our farms." Burx walked up in front of Thrall's throne, his face so close that his and Thrall's tusks almost touched. "It *fits*, Warchief. And you know it."

In a low tone, Thrall said, "What I know, Burx, is that Lady Proudmoore stood against her own father rather than destroy the alliance between Durotar and Theramore. Do you truly think she would abandon it now over *trees*?"

Burx backed off, throwing up his arms. "Who can say how humans think?"

"*I* can. As you were so quick to point out before, Burx, I was raised with humans—I have seen both the best and the worst humanity has to offer. And I can tell you now that, while there are most definitely humans who *would* do this, Jaina Proudmoore is *not* one of them."

Folding his arms defiantly in front of his chest, Burx said, "There aren't any other human mages on Kalimdor that we know about. Who's that leave, Warchief?"

"I do not know." Thrall smiled. "When Lieutenant Blackmoore had me educated like a human, he had me read many philosophical and scientific treatises. Something that stood out in those lessons was one comment—that the beginning of wisdom is the statement 'I do not know.' The person who cannot make that statement is one who will never learn anything. And I have prided myself on my ability to learn, Burx." He stood again. "Send warriors to Drygulch. Try to corral the thunder lizards. Provide whatever aid they need to bring this problem under control." Then he faced Kaltnar. "Fetch the talisman. I would speak to Lady Proudmoore."

"We should take *action!*" Burx stomped his foot again, even as Kalthar slowly walked out of the room to do as Thrall had instructed. "We should not be *talking.*"

"Talking is the second step to learning things, Burx. I intend to learn who was responsible for this. Now go and follow my instructions."

Burx started to say something, but Thrall would not let him.

"There will be no more from you, Burx! You have made your position *quite* clear! However, I think even you will agree that the needs of Drygulch are more immediate. Now go and do as I have said before our farms truly *are* devastated."

"Of course, Warchief," Burx said. He saluted as the boy had, and then departed.

Thrall hoped that his defense of Jaina was earned. In his heart, he knew it was. But if Jaina Proudmoore did not steal their trees and let loose the thunder lizards—who did?

EIGHT

Lorena was led into Lady Proudmoore's chambers by Duree, that lunatic old woman who managed the lady's affairs, only to find that the room was empty.

Whirling on Duree, over whom she loomed by a full head, Lorena said, "Where is she?"

"She'll be back soon, stop your fretting. It's been an hour since she went off to meet with that orc Warchief—oughta be back any moment now."

Frowning, Lorena asked, "She's meeting with Thrall?"

Putting her hand to her mouth, Duree said, "Oh dear, I wasn't supposed to mention that. Just forget I said anything, will you please, dear?"

The colonel said nothing, instead twisting her square face into a snarl designed with the express purpose of getting the old woman out of the chambers.

At that, it succeeded rather admirably, as Duree

dashed from the chambers, her spectacles falling off her nose.

A moment later, Kristoff entered. "Colonel. Duree said you had a report."

Lorena looked at the chamberlain. Like the old woman, Kristoff was a necessary evil—after all, a nation did not run on soldiering alone. One of the first lessons her father and brothers had taught her was to be good to the clerks and the like. They were the people who kept any unit functioning, far more than any high-ranking officers.

She found Duree so annoying that she did not put that advice to good use with her, but Kristoff was the lady's right hand. So Lorena put aside her intense dislike for the man himself and forced a smile onto her face.

"Yes, Chamberlain, I have a report for the lady, which I'll give her as soon as she arrives."

Kristoff smiled. It was the most insincere smile Lorena had ever seen, and after spending years guarding the keep at Kul Tiras, it was against some stiff competition. "You may give it to me, and I can assure you that I will pass it on to Lady Proudmoore."

"I prefer to wait for milady myself, sir, if you don't mind."

"She is away on official business." Kristoff inhaled sharply. "She could be some time."

Giving the chamberlain an insincere smile of her own, the colonel said, "The lady's a mage—when her business is conducted, she'll be back in an instant. And she wished me to report directly to her."

"Colonel—"

Whatever Kristoff was about to say was lost to a loud popping sound and a flash of light that heralded the arrival of Lady Proudmoore.

She wasn't much to look at, the colonel had always thought, but she had also learned early on that mages were not ones to judge on appearances. Lorena had spent all her life trying to make herself look as male as possible—keeping her hair cut short, not shaving her legs, wearing undergarments that hid her breasts—and even with all that, she was often dismissed as being "just" a woman. It amazed Lorena how this small, pale woman with her golden hair and deep blue eyes managed to gain the respect of so many.

In part, Lorena supposed it was the way she carried herself. She seemed to be the tallest person in whatever room she stood in, even though she was often the shortest. Her clothes all tended to be white: boots, blouse, pantaloons, cloak. Most amazingly, the clothes *remained* a shiny white. It took a week out of every year of a soldier's life to keep the white trim in the plate armor from turning brown or gray, and most were unsuccessful, yet Lady Proudmoore's clothes almost glowed.

Lorena supposed that was a fortuitous side effect of being a powerful mage.

"Colonel, you've returned." Lady Proudmoore

spoke as if she'd been standing in the room all along. "Please report."

Quickly and concisely, Lorena told the lady, as well as the chamberlain, what she and her people had learned at Northwatch.

Kristoff pursed his thin lips. "I've never heard of this Burning Blade."

"I have." The lady had flipped back her hood, letting her golden curls loose, and sat at her desk while Lorena was giving her report, and she now put a finger to her chin. "There was an orc clan by that name, but they've been wiped out. And some of the Elite Guard have mentioned it in passing."

Lorena didn't like the sound of this. It was one thing for Strov to have heard of it, but if rumors of this organization were reaching the lady's personal guards, then something was amiss. "These were orcs, ma'am, that much I'm sure of."

"Or were made to look like orcs," Lady Proudmoore said. "They obviously had use of magic—which is vexing enough—and therefore could have been deliberately masking themselves. After all, an unprovoked attack on human soldiers by orcs would do much to destabilize our alliance."

"It is also possible," Kristoff said, "that these are orc agitators who are using this extinct clan for their own purposes."

Lorena shook her head. "That doesn't explain how Private Strov's brother heard of them in a Theramore tavern."

The lady nodded, her thoughts seeming to turn inward, as if she forgot there were others in the room. Lorena had known few wizards in her time, but they all had a tendency to wander mentally.

However, unlike those other mages—who often needed a club to the head to pay attention to the world around them—Lady Proudmoore usually was able to bring herself back to reality on her own. She did so now, and stood up. "Colonel, I want you to investigate this Burning Blade. We need to know who they are, how they operate, especially if they're using magic. If they have orc recruits, then why try to lure humans? Get to the bottom of it, Lorena—use whoever you need."

Standing straight, Lorena saluted. "Yes, ma'am."

"Kristoff, I'm afraid I'm going to need to depart immediately. Thunder lizards have gotten loose from Thunder Ridge, and are endangering Drygulch Ravine."

Frowning, the chamberlain said, "I fail to see how that concerns us—or you."

"A section of the forest that keeps the lizards contained in the ridge has been razed to the stump. Orcs did *not* do that."

"How can you be sure of that?" Kristoff sounded incredulous.

Lorena felt much the same way at the chamberlain's idiotic words. "It can't possibly have been orcs." Realizing she spoke out of turn, she shot Lady Proudmoore a look. "I'm sorry, ma'am."

Smiling, the lady said, "Quite all right. Please, continue."

Looking back at Kristoff, Lorena said, "Even when they were cursed by the Burning Legion, orcs would *never* do such a thing. Orcs have always had a reverence for the land that, frankly, borders on the psychotic."

Lady Proudmoore chuckled. "Actually, I'd say that the human proclivity for abuse of nature is what borders on the psychotic, but the colonel's point is well taken. Orcs simply aren't capable of doing that—especially given what would happen with the thunder lizards. That leaves the trolls, who have ceded themselves to Thrall's rule, the goblins, who are neutral, and us—allies of Durotar." She sighed. "In addition, there is no sign of the lumber that was cut down. It had to have been transported, but there are no reports of any convoys, by air or land. Which means magic."

Not liking the sound of that at all, Lorena asked, "Ma'am, do you believe the Burning Blade had something to do with it?"

"After hearing your report, Colonel, I'm very much inclined in that direction—and that's what I want you to learn."

Kristoff folded his spindly arms over his small chest. "I fail to see how this requires your being away from Theramore."

"I promised Thrall I would investigate personally." She smiled wryly. "Right now, I'm his best suspect for performing this act, since cutting down the trees and teleporting them elsewhere on Kalimdor is well within my abilities. What better way to prove my innocence than to learn the truth myself?"

"I can think of several ways," Kristoff said sourly.

Lady Proudmoore walked around to the other side of her desk, standing face to face with her chamberlain. "There is another reason. It is quite possible that magic is afoot here. Powerful magic. If there is magic of this much power on Kalimdor, I need to know who is wielding it—and learn why the mage in question has remained secretive."

"*If* magic is involved." Kristoff sounded so petulant Lorena wanted desperately to punch him. However, he then let out a long breath and unfolded his arms. "Still, I suppose that *is* a legitimate concern. At the very least, it does need to be investigated. I withdraw my objections."

Dryly, the lady said, "I'm *so* glad you approve, Kristoff." She walked back to her desk, rummaging through the pile of scrolls. "I will depart in the morning. Kristoff, you will handle things while I'm gone, as I'm not sure how long this will take. You will be empowered to act in my name until my return." Turning toward Lorena, she added, "Good hunting, Colonel. You're both dismissed."

Lorena saluted again, turned on her heel, and departed. As she exited, she heard Kristoff start to say something, but the lady interrupted. "I *said* you were dismissed, Chamberlain."

"Of course, ma'am."

The colonel couldn't help but smile at the peeved tone in the chamberlain's voice.

There were times when Jaina Proudmoore really hated being right.

Being wrong was never something that bothered her, and she mostly blamed Antonidas for that. Her mentor had drummed into her from the moment her apprenticeship started that the worst sin a mage could commit was arrogance, and also the easiest. "With so much power at your command—literally at your fingertips—it is easy to be tempted to think that you are *all*-powerful," the older wizard had said. "Indeed it is so easy that most wizards succumb to the notion. It is one of the reasons why we are often so tiresome." That last had been said with a small smile.

"You're not like that, though, are you?" Jaina had asked.

"All too regularly," had been the mage's reply. "The trick is to recognize the flaw in yourself and work to correct it." Then her mentor had told her of mages past, such as Aegwynn and Medivh, the last two Guardians of Tirisfal, both of whom had let their arrogance be their downfall. Years later, Jaina would work alongside Medivh and see that he at least had redeemed himself. His mother, Aegwynn, was less fortunate. The first female Guardian—and someone Jaina had admired for most of her life—her one mistake in her centuries as Guardian was to believe herself to have defeated Sargeras. In fact, she destroyed only his avatar, and allowed the demon to hide within her soul, remaining there for centuries until Aegwynn sired Medivh, and then Sargeras moved to him. Medivh had been the vessel for Sargeras's invasion, and for the orcs' presence in this world, all because Aegwynn was arrogant enough to believe that she could have defeated Sargeras alone.

Jaina had taken those words to heart, and so always doubted her own surety. She still admired Aegwynn— without her blazing the trail, the only response to Jaina's attempts to study magic would have been laughter, instead of the swayable skepticism she was met with. And she had swayed Antonidas.

Sometimes that self-doubt worked against her—she hadn't listened to her instinct that Arthas had turned for far longer than was wise, given Arthas's descent, and she always wondered if things would have been different if she'd acted sooner. But mostly, that had served her well. It also made her, she hoped, a wise leader to the people of Theramore.

When Thrall had told her of the destruction of a section of the forest that surrounded Thunder Ridge, she had known immediately that magic was at work, and powerful magic at that. She had hoped, however, that she was wrong in that assumption.

That turned out to be a forlorn hope. She went straight to the forest in question from her chambers in Theramore, and as soon as she materialized, she could practically smell the magic. Indeed, even without her magically enhanced abilities, she'd have known that magic was afoot here. Before her was a range of stumps, stretching almost as far as a human could see, before disappearing over the hill that led down to the ridge. The top of each stump was on a perfectly straight line with all the surrounding ones—it was as if a giant saw had gone through all the trees at once. More to the point, the cuts were all completely even, with no flaws or breaks. One could attain such a level of perfection only with magic.

Jaina knew most of the mages who still lived. The few besides herself who were capable of this were not on Kalimdor. What's more, this magic didn't have the feel of any of those she knew. Every wizard wielded the forces of magic differently, and if one was sensitive enough, one could tell the differences from one mage to the next. This felt like no mage Jaina knew. And it gave her a mildly nauseous feeling, which led her to think that it might well be demonic magic. The nausea didn't necessarily mean demonic magic, of course, though the presence of the Burning Legion's wizardry had always made Jaina ill. But so had Kel'Thuzad's when Antonidas first introduced them in the third year of Jaina's apprenticeship, and that was when the archmage was one of the finest mages in Kirin Tor (long before he turned to necromancy and became a servant of the Lich King).

Besides which, the source of the destruction was of less import than its result: thunder lizards were now roaming unfettered through Drygulch, and possibly beyond. Jaina needed to find a remote place to relocate them where they wouldn't rampage all over the farms and cities the orcs had built here.

Reaching under her cloak, she pulled out the map, one of two items she had taken off the mess on her desk. She had decided upon the Bladescar Highlands as the ideal place to relocate the lizards. Located in the southern portion of Durotar, due east of Ratchet, the highlands were remote, separated from the rest of Durotar by mountains that the thunder lizards would be hard-pressed to navigate. Plus, the region had plenty of grasslands for them to graze, room for them to stampede to their heart's content, and a mountain stream that was almost as big as the river they had use of in Thunder Ridge. The lizards would be safe, and so would the population of Durotar.

Her initial thought was to move them even farther away—say to Feralas on the other side of the continent—but even Jaina's abilities had their limits. She could teleport herself there easily enough, but herself and hundreds of thunder lizards was more than even she could handle over such a distance.

She then removed the other item from her cloak—a scroll containing a spell that would enable her to sense the mind of any thunder lizard on the continent. She spoke the incantation and then cast her senses outward. Unlike most reptiles, thunder lizards had a herd mentality akin to that of cattle, so most of them had stayed together even as they departed their home. Sure enough, she found the bulk of them milling around the river that fed Drygulch Ravine. They were in a docile phase right now, which simplified Jaina's life considerably. She was prepared to magically put them into such a phase if need be. Thunder lizards were either docile or stampeding—they didn't really have much of a middle ground, and teleporting them while stampeding would be a good deal more problematic. Still, she preferred not to disturb the animals' routine any more than necessary, so she was glad they were in the more cooperative mode.

For a caster to include anyone but herself in the teleportation spell required line of sight—at least, according to most scrolls one would find on the subject. However, Antonidas had told Jaina that one could also do it if one was in what he called "line of mind." It required the mage to reach out and touch the thoughts of whomever she wished to teleport. This was a lot riskier, as there were many whose minds were difficult or dangerous to touch. Other mages and demons generally had protections against such things, and even someone particularly strong-willed would probably be able to resist.

No such impediment existed with the thunder lizards, however. Right now, their minds were focused on one of three things: eating, drinking, or sleeping. In addition to running very fast, those activities were generally all that occupied a thunder lizard's mind, except during mating season.

Still and all, it took several hours for Jaina, standing in

the razed forest, to reach out with her mind to each thunder lizard in Drygulch, as well as the stragglers that had wandered off toward Razor Hill.

Grass. Water. Eyes close. Rest. Lap up. Chew. Swallow. Sip. Sleep. Breathe.

For a moment, she was almost lost—true, the lizards' thought patterns weren't complex, but there were *hundreds* of them, and she found herself overwhelmed by their instinctive need to eat and drink and sleep.

Gritting her teeth, she reasserted her own self over that of hundreds of thunder lizards. She then started to mutter the incantation for the teleport spell.

Pain! Searing white-hot agony sliced through Jaina's skull as soon as she uttered the final syllable of the spell. The ruined forest melted before her and then slammed back into form immediately. A milder pain shot through Jaina's left knee, and only then did she realize that she had stumbled to the ground, her knee colliding with the nearest stump.

Pain. Hurt. Hurt. Hurt. Run. Run. Run. Run. No more pain. Run, no pain.

Sweat beading on her forehead, Jaina resisted the urge to start running through the forest. Something happened to the teleport spell, but Jaina couldn't take the time to find out what just yet, because the pain she felt when the spell was ruined was transferred to the thunder lizards via their mental link. It was serving to put them into a stampeding frame of mind, and she had to stop them before they ran through Drygulch again.

Every instinct screamed for her to break the link, as holding back the urges of the now-agitated lizards was like trying to hold back the ocean with a broom. But the only way to calm them was to keep the link. Closing her eyes and forcing herself to focus, she cast a spell that Antonidas had said was specifically written to calm bucking mounts. Clenching her fists so hard she feared her fingernails would draw blood, she shoved as much of herself as she could into the spell, making sure to catch all the lizards with it.

Moments later they were all asleep. Jaina barely managed to break the mental link before she herself also succumbed. Her own fatigue was doing enough without adding the lizards' magically induced naps.

Her limbs ached, and her eyelids felt heavy. Teleport spells were draining under the best of circumstances, and both the volume she was trying to move and the spell's violent end made these circumstances far from the best. Jaina wanted nothing more than to lie down and join the lizards in their slumber, but she couldn't afford that. The spell would only keep the lizards asleep for six hours—possibly less because the spell was so diffuse. She had to find out what there was in Bladescar that kept her from completing the spell.

She sat, folding her legs together, letting her hands fall limply to her side, and controlled her breathing. Then she once again cast her senses outward, this time toward the Bladescar range, specifically the small area in the center of the mountainous region.

It didn't take her long to find what she was looking for.

Someone had put up wards around the entire highlands. From this distance, Jaina could not pinpoint the type of magic being used, but the wards were precisely the type designed to—among other things—disrupt teleportation spells in order to keep whatever was inside the wards protected.

Jaina stood and collected herself. She was about to start the teleportation spell that would bring her to Bladescar, then stopped herself. Reaching into the small pack attached to her belt, she took out some jerky. Another of Antonidas's earliest lessons was a reminder that magic used the body, and the only way to replenish the body was to consume food. "More wizards," he had said, "have wasted away because they were so busy exploring the wonders of magic that they forgot to *eat.*"

Her jaw aching from chewing the tough dried meat, the newly refreshed Jaina then cast the spell that would take her to a spot just outside the wards placed around the highlands.

The one flaw in her plan to eat before teleporting was that the stomach rumblings she often felt as a side effect of the spell were far more pronounced with undigested food still in her belly. But she pushed past the effect as she stood on the steep incline that more or less demarcated the beginning of the highlands. Below and behind her was a sheer cliff. In front of her was the slanted grasslands. There was barely enough room to stand.

Of course, the wards were invisible to the naked eye. But Jaina could nonetheless feel them. They were not particularly powerful, but they didn't really need to be. In fact, if the object was to hide someone or something—which Jaina was becoming more and more convinced was the case here—it was best to keep the wards at a low level. Too powerful, and they would be like a beacon to any mage.

This close, Jaina also recognized the flavor of the magic that had cast these wards. She last felt it in the company of Medivh, during the war. This was *Tirisfalen* magic—but all the Guardians were supposed to be dead, including Medivh, the last of them.

Removing the wards—now that she knew they were there—was but the work of a gesture. She then walked ahead and started to explore the highlands, pausing to put a concealment spell on herself so she could move about undetected.

At first, it was just as she expected: grasslands, dotted with fruit-bearing bushes and the occasional tree. A wind blew in off the Great Sea, funneled by the mountains and billowing Jaina's white cloak behind her. It had been cloudy back at Thunder Ridge, but the highlands were above the cloud line, so it was bright and sunny here. Jaina cast her cloak's hood back so she could enjoy the feeling of the sun on her face.

Soon she came across the first sign of whatever was

hiding: several of the bushes had had their fruit picked recently. As she continued to walk uphill, she found a well that had been built, with some firewood stacked next to it. On the other side of a large tree, she saw a large hut. Rows of plants—vegetables, mostly, and some spices—were planted in an orderly manner in an area behind the hut that was more or less level.

A moment later, a woman came into view. She was dressed only in a threadbare light blue linen dress; her feet were bare. Her gait was steady, and as she approached the well, Jaina saw that she was unusually tall for a woman—certainly taller than Jaina herself. In addition, she was unmistakably old. Wrinkles marred her face, which Jaina thought must once have been beautiful. The woman had white hair held in place with a tarnished silver diadem, and the deepest green eyes Jaina had ever seen. They matched the cracked jade pendant she wore around her neck.

Suddenly, the hairs on the back of Jaina's neck stood on end, as she thought she recognized the woman. They had never met, of course, but she'd read descriptions during her apprenticeship, and all the accounts made mention of her great height, her blond hair held simply with a silver diadem—and her eyes. Everyone was sure to mention those jade eyes.

Certainly, if it was her, it explained the wards. Yet she was supposed to have died long ago. . . .

The woman put her hands on her hips. "I know you're there, so you might as well not waste that concealment spell." She shook her head as she moved to the well and lowered a bucket by letting down the rope hand over hand. "Honestly, they don't teach you young mages *anything* these days. Violet Citadel's gone to pot, and that's the truth."

Jaina dropped the concealment. The woman barely reacted beyond making a *tsk* noise while lowering the rope.

"My name is Lady Jaina Proudmoore. I rule Theramore, the human city on this continent."

"Good for you. When you get back to this Theramore place, work on that concealment spell. Couldn't hide from a bloodhound with a cold with that thing."

Her mind reeling, Jaina realized that this woman couldn't possibly be anyone *but* who she thought it was, impossible as that might have been. "Magna, it's an honor to meet you. I had thought that you were—"

"Dead?" The woman snorted as she started pulling the rope back up, her mouth showing the signs of the greater strain of lifting a water-filled bucket. "I *am* dead, Lady Jaina Proudmoore of Theramore—or as close as makes no never mind. And don't go calling me 'Magna.' That was another time and another place, and I'm not that woman anymore."

"The title is not one you lose, Magna. And I cannot bring myself to call you anything else."

"Balderdash. If you're gonna call me anything, call me by my name. Call me Aegwynn."

NINE

For many years, Rexxar, last of the Mok'Nathal Clan, walked the continent of Kalimdor alone, save for the company of the big brown bear, Misha. Born of orc and ogre blood both, as most of his now-defunct clan, he had grown weary of the squabbling and ruthlessness and endless war that characterized what was laughingly referred to as civilization. In truth, Rexxar found more civilization in Misha's fellow bears or the wolves of Winterspring than in any of the human, dwarven, elven, or troll cities that marred the landscape.

No, Rexxar preferred to wander, living off the land, and being answerable to none. If he ever felt the urge to call a place home, he knew that he had one in Durotar. During the founding of the orc nation, Rexxar had come to the aid of a dying orc who was charged with bringing a message to Thrall. Granting the warrior his final wish, Rexxar had brought Thrall the report, and found himself amid orcs who had gone back to the old ways, before Gul'dan and his Shadow Council destroyed a once-great people.

But, though Rexxar was honored to call Thrall a comrade and swear fealty to him, and was happy to fulfill that oath by aiding the orcs against Admiral Proudmoore's treachery, among other services, in the end, Rexxar preferred to wander. Even as great a nation as Durotar had towns and settlements and order. Rexxar was built for the chaos of the wild.

Without warning, Misha broke into a run.

Hesitating for but a second, Rexxar followed his companion. He couldn't hope to keep up with the four-legged animal's loping gait, of course, but the half-breed's powerful legs were enough to keep him within sight of her. Misha wouldn't bolt from her companion's side without good reason.

They were in a region near the coast, filled with high grass. Though lesser beings might have found the terrain difficult to cross, Rexxar and Misha had sufficient strength to bend the grasses to their will.

It was only a minute later that Misha came to a halt, her snout invisible as it dipped into the shoulder-high blades. Rexxar slowed down and put his hand to the hilt of one of the axes strapped to his back.

What he found—what Misha had scented—was the body of a full-blooded orc. Rexxar knew this because a considerable amount of its blood had been shed.

His hands falling to his side, Rexxar shook his head.

"A fallen warrior. It is only a pity that he died alone, without comrades to aid him in battle."

Before the half-breed wanderer could contemplate putting the brave orc's soul to rest, he heard a whisper.

"Not . . . dead . . . yet . . ."

Misha made a yowling noise, as if surprised that the orc could speak. Peering down closely at what he had believed to be a corpse, Rexxar saw that the orc had lost an eye. The dead socket was healed over, so the wound had not been inflicted by the same hand—or hands— that had brought him to the brink now.

"Burning . . . Blade . . . must . . . get . . . to . . . Orgrimmar. Thrall . . . warned. Burning . . . Blade . . ."

Rexxar knew not what was so important about a blade that burned, but this warrior was obviously clinging to life only because he had yet to provide the necessary intelligence to Thrall. Recalling the oath he had sworn to the Warchief, Rexxar asked, "What is your name?"

"By—Byrok."

"Fear not, noble Byrok. I am Rexxar of the Mok'-Nathal, and I swear to you that Misha and I will see you brought to Orgrimmar to deliver your warning to the Warchief."

"Rexxar . . . you . . . are known . . . to me . . . We . . . must . . . make haste . . ."

The half-breed could not say the same of this Byrok, but it mattered not. With a gentleness he rarely had cause to employ, he lifted Byrok's bleeding form and lay him across Misha's expansive back. The bear bore the weight with no protest—though they had sworn no actual oath, the bond between Rexxar and Misha was unbreakable. If Rexxar desired it, Misha would do it.

Without another word, they turned westward toward Orgrimmar.

The first time Rexxar came to Orgrimmar, it was still being built. Around him had been many dozens of orcs building structures, clearing pathways, and transforming the harsh wilderness of Kalimdor into a home.

Upon his return now, that work had been done, but there were still many dozens of orcs visible through the gates, engaged in the day-to-day business of life. Though he had little use for civilization, Rexxar did feel pride and joy in what he saw. Since coming to this world, his mother's people had either been cursed tools of Gul'dan's demonic masters or broken slaves of their human enemies. If orcs were to live in this world, better it be on their own terms.

Surrounded on three sides by hills, a massive stone wall had been built on the city's fourth side. Reinforced with giant wooden logs, the wall was broken only by a large wooden gate, currently open, and two wooden watchtowers. Atop the wall were more logs, sharpened to a point to discourage enemies from storming the gates, and poles with pointed ends. The crimson flag of the Horde hung from both towers and from some of the poles.

It was, Rexxar thought, a fearsome sight, fitting for the home of the mightiest warriors in the world.

A guard wielding a spear approached from the gate. "Who goes there?"

"I am Rexxar, last son of the Mok'Nathal. I bear Byrok, who has been injured, and carries a message for Warchief Thrall."

The guard scowled, then looked up at one of the watchtowers. The warrior stationed there yelled down, "It's all right, I remember that one—and his bear. Know that wolf's-head mask anywhere. He's a friend to the Warchief. Let him in!" Rexxar wore the hollowed-out head of a wolf he had slain on his crown. It served as protection for his head and an image of fear for his enemies.

Satisfied with that, the guard stepped aside, allowing Rexxar, Misha, and the bear's burden to enter Orgrimmar.

The orc city was built within a huge ravine, with traditional hexagonal structures built into the sides of the ravine as well as the recesses. As he walked through the Valley of Honor, where the gate was built, toward the Valley of Wisdom, where Thrall's throne room was housed, Rexxar was both fascinated and appalled. The former because the orcs had come so far in a mere three summers. The latter because it was yet another city in a world that had too many of them already.

When he was about halfway to the Valley of Wisdom, he was met by the familiar site of a medium-height orc: Nazgrel, the head of Thrall's security, along with four of his guards. "Greetings, last son of the Mok'Nathal. It has been far too long."

Out of respect, Rexxar removed his headgear. "Since seeing you, Nazgrel, yes—since being in the city, no. But I did swear an oath to Thrall, and I would not leave this noble warrior to die in the grass."

Nazgrel nodded. "We have come to escort you to him—and the shaman has been summoned as well, to tend to Byrok. We've also come to relieve Misha of her burden." At a gesture from Nazgrel, two of the guards lifted the bleeding form of Byrok from Misha's back. At first, the bear started a growl, but at a look from Rexxar, she backed down.

They proceeded through the long and winding roads of Orgrimmar to the large hexagonal building at the far side of the Valley of Wisdom. Thrall was waiting for him in the throne room, which Rexxar found to be as cold as Frostsaber Rock. Thrall sat on his throne, with the wizened shaman Kalthar standing on one side of the throne, and an orc Rexxar did not know on the other. When the guards had placed Byrok on the floor in front of the throne, Kalthar moved to kneel at the warrior's side.

Shivering slightly, Rexxar saluted the Warchief. "I bid you greetings, Warchief of the Horde."

Thrall smiled. "It is very good to see you again, my friend—I only wish it would not take one of my people being beaten to near-death to bring you back to Orgrimmar's gates."

"It is not my way to live among city-dwellers, Warchief—as you well know."

"Indeed, I do. Still, you have again done us a great service." He turned to the shaman. "How is he?"

"He will survive—he is a strong one. And he wishes to speak."

"Can he?" Thrall asked.

Kalthar sniffed. "Not well, but I doubt he will allow me to treat him properly until he does."

"I must . . . sit up . . . Help me, shaman." That was Byrok. He sounded stronger than he had in the grasses, but not by much.

With a huge sigh, the wizened orc gestured to Nazgrel's guards, who helped Byrok into a sitting position.

Hesitatingly, pausing many times for breath, Byrok spoke of what happened to him. Rexxar knew nothing of the Burning Blade, but the others did, apparently—it was an old orc clan.

"This can't be the same thing," the orc Rexxar did not know said.

"It does seem unlikely, it's true, Burx," Thrall said, "but if their symbol is the same—"

Burx shook his head. "It could be a coincidence, but I don't buy that. Besides, I've been hearing rumors about a human cult that's been building up in Theramore. They're called the Flaming Sword. It might be that one of them had some of our people as slaves, learned of the symbol that way, and took it for their own use."

Nazgrel nodded. "I've heard some of those rumors as well, Warchief."

"With respect," Kalthar said, "I must treat this man. He has discharged his duty, now I must take him from this ridiculously cold throne room and heal him."

"Of course." Thrall nodded, and, at the old shaman's direction, the guards took Byrok out of the throne room.

Thrall then got up from his animal-skin throne and started to pace. "What do you know of this Flaming Sword, Nazgrel?"

Nazgrel shrugged. "Very little—humans gathering in their homes to talk about things."

Burx sneered. "Sitting and talking are things the humans do *quite* well."

"But if they are brash enough to attack an orc within Durotar's borders," Nazgrel added, "then they've become a lot more powerful than we thought."

"We've got to respond," Burx said. "It's only a matter of time before the humans attack us."

Rexxar thought this extreme. "You would condemn an entire species on the actions of six of them?"

"They'd do the same to us in a heartbeat," Burx said. "And unless these are the same six who stole our trees, and who stood around and did nothing while orc traders were attacked, then it is very much *more* than six people."

Thrall turned to face Burx. "Theramore is our ally, Burx. Jaina would not allow such a thing to gain power."

"She may not have any control over this," Nazgrel

said. "For all her power, for all she has earned our respect, she is but one human female."

Rexxar remembered Jaina Proudmoore as the only honorable human he'd ever met. When faced with a choice between siding with her father, her very flesh and blood, and honoring a promise to an orc, she chose the latter. That choice saved Durotar from being destroyed before it was finished. "The Lady Proudmoore," he said, "will do what is right."

Shaking his head, Burx said, "Your confidence is touching, Mok'Nathal, but misplaced. Do you really think that a *woman* can change decades of human evil? They fought us and killed us and *enslaved* us! Do you think that will change just because one person says so?"

"The orcs changed because one person said so," Rexxar said quietly. "That person stands before you now as Warchief. Do you doubt him?"

At that, Burx backed down. "Of course not. But—"

Thrall, however, had obviously made his decision. He sat back down on the throne, refusing to let Burx finish. "I know what Jaina is capable of, and I know her heart. She will not betray us, and if there are vipers in her midst, both the Horde and the most powerful wizard on the continent will deal with it *together*. When she has finished with the thunder lizards, I will speak to her of this Flaming Sword." He turned and looked right at Burx. "What we will *not* do is go back on our word to the humans and attack. Is that clear?"

"Yes, Warchief."

TEN

Strov had been sitting in a dark corner of the Demonsbane Inn and Tavern for an hour when his brother Manuel walked in with four of his fellow dockworkers.

At Colonel Lorena's direction, Strov had spoken with his brother about the Burning Blade. Manuel said he hadn't seen the person who tried to recruit him since that first time, but the last few times he'd gone to the Demonsbane, he'd overheard a weaselly little fisherman named Margoz mutter to himself about the Burning Blade, usually after consuming several corn whiskeys. Strov had been hoping for the original recruiter Manuel had told him of weeks earlier, but Manuel insisted that the man hadn't appeared at the Demonsbane since.

Manuel had never been any good at describing people; the best he could do regarding Margoz was "weaselly," and that word described half the Demonsbane's patronage. But Manuel insisted that he could find the man again if he saw him, and said he would come to the Demonsbane after his shift on the docks was done.

Strov arrived early, taking a seat in the corner, wanting to blend into the background of the tavern and people-watch. After a few hours, he decided that he had no desire to ever patronize this establishment again. The table was filthy, and the stool he sat on was uneven and rocked on the unswept floor. He got his first drink—a watery ale—at the bar, and no attempt had been made to refill it. It amazed Strov that the owner could stay in business.

On top of that, Strov found the demon skull behind the bar to be incredibly disturbing. It was as if the thing were staring right at him the entire time. Although, thinking on it, he could see how the presence of that skull looming over everyone in the tavern would drive people to drink more, so he supposed that, at least, was a sound business decision.

Manuel came in with a bunch of men who, like him, were burly and loud and wearing only sleeveless shirts and loose cotton pants. Strov's brother earned his daily bread loading and unloading ships docked in Theramore, and then spent most of it either at dice or in this tavern. It was work that challenged only the body, not the mind, which was why it had held no interest for Strov, but held plenty for the much less imaginative Manuel. Strov's older brother wasn't one to think overmuch on things. Even the soldier's training Strov had received when he enlisted would have been too taxing for him. He preferred the simplicity of being told to take a box from one place and put it in another place. Anything more than that—like the intricacies of fighting with a sword—gave him a headache.

As the dockworkers made their way inside the bar, Manuel said, "Find a table, fellas, I'll be orderin' the drinks."

"First round on you?" one of his coworkers asked with a grin.

"You wish—we'll divvy up later." Manuel laughed and walked up to the bar. Strov noted that his brother didn't move in a straight line to the bar, but instead took an odd angle so he had to squeeze in between two other people in order to stand at the bar. "Evenin', Erik," he said to the barkeep.

The barkeep just nodded.

"Two ales, one corn whiskey, one wine, and a boar's grog."

Strov smiled. Manuel always had a weakness for boar's grog, which was of course the most expensive item in the tavern. This was one of several reasons why he still lived with their parents while Strov had his own place.

"The usual," Erik said. "Comin' up."

As Erik went to put the order together, Manuel turned to look at the man seated next to him. He'd arrived after Strov did, but was already on his third corn whiskey. "Hey," Manuel said, "you're Margoz, right?"

The man just looked up and stared blankly at Manuel.

"You're with them Burning Blade folk, right? Had a fella in here awhile back, was lookin' for recruits. You're with 'em, yeah?"

"Dunno what you're talking about." Margoz's words were sufficiently slurred that his consonants barely qualified as such. " 'Scuse me."

Margoz then got off his stool, stumbled to the floor, got up while refusing assistance from Manuel, and then walked very slowly and unsteadily toward the door.

A moment later, after Manuel gave him a look and a nod, Strov abandoned his long-empty mug and also exited onto the streets of Theramore.

The cobblestone streets that formed a lattice amid the buildings of Theramore were designed to provide reinforced ground for people, mounts, and wheeled conveyances to travel without risking getting mired in the swampy ground the city had been built on. Most people walked on them rather than the muck and grass on either side, which meant the thoroughfares were so crowded that Strov could follow Margoz without fear of being noticed.

After Margoz bumped into four different people, two of whom actively tried to avoid him, Strov realized that they could have been alone on the street for all it mattered. Margoz was so drunk he wouldn't have noticed a dragon following him down the street.

Still, Strov refused to let his training go to waste, so he kept a good distance behind and rarely looked right at the target, though he kept him in his peripheral vision.

They soon arrived at a small adobe structure near the docks. This particular house was constructed of the cheaper material rather than wood or stone, indicating that very poor people indeed lived here. If this Margoz was a fisherman, as Manuel thought, he was obviously a bad one, as it took a true lack of skill to not succeed as a fisherman on an island on the coast of the Great Sea. The nearest cesspool was poorly concealed, and Strov almost gagged from the odor of waste in the air.

Margoz entered the building, which was probably originally constructed as a four-room house, but now had each room rented out to a different tenant. Strov took up position behind a tree across the way from it.

Three of the rooms already had lanterns burning. The fourth lit up about half a minute after Margoz entered. Strov casually walked across the way and then stood near Margoz's window, making as if to urinate on the wall. He made sure to stumble as he approached, so that any passersby would assume he was drunk. It wasn't all that unusual late at night to see drunks relieving themselves on whatever surface presented itself.

From Margoz's room, Strov heard the words: "*Galtak Ered'nash. Ered'nash ban galar. Ered'nash havik yrthog. Galtak Ered'nash.*"

Strov started. He didn't recognize the rest of it, but the first and last part were things the orcs who attacked them at Northwatch had said.

Pleased with himself for having rightly made this connection, Strov continued listening.

Then his entire face scrunched up in revulsion at the sudden stink of sulfur. On the face of it, sulfur should have been more pleasant, or at least less revolting, than the cesspool's overwhelming odor. But there was something wrong—something *evil*—about this smell. Margoz's words had sounded like an incantation, and now this. Not only was magic afoot, but Strov was willing to bet his sword that it was demonic magic.

" 'M sorry, sir, I didn' mean to—" Margoz paused. "Yeah, I realize y'don' wanna be bothered 'less it's important, but it's been *months*, sir, and 'm still in 'is same hole. I jus' wanna know—" Another pause. "Well, it's importan' t'*me*! And wha's more, people keep *talkin'* t'me, like I can help 'em or somethin'."

Strov couldn't hear the other half of the conversation, which meant that either Margoz was crazy and was talking to himself—which Strov had to admit was likely, especially given his inebriated state—or the other half of the conversation was meant for Margoz's ears only.

"I dunno whatcher talkin' 'bout. Nobody didn'—" Another pause. "Well, how's *I* s'posed t'know that? Huh? I ain't got eyes'n the back'a my head!"

What Strov knew about demons was mostly how to kill them, but this odd one-sided conversation definitely had the stink of demon to Strov—and not just because of the sulfur.

He did up his pants. At this point, he had enough to report to Colonel Lorena. Besides, he didn't much like the idea of being this close to a demon.

Turning around, he found himself facing absolute darkness.

"What the—?" He whirled around, but there was only darkness behind him as well. Theramore had completely disappeared.

I do not like spies.

Strov didn't so much hear the voice as *feel* it in his very bones. It was as if someone had sewn his eyes shut, only his eyes were open, but he couldn't see *anything*.

No, it wasn't just sight that had gone quiet. The darkness extended to his other senses. He could no longer hear the bustle of Theramore, nor taste the salty air, nor feel the breeze wafting in off the Great Sea.

And the only thing he smelled now was sulfur.

Why do you spy on my minion?

Strov said nothing. He wasn't sure he was capable of speech, and even if he was, he would never give up information to a creature such as this.

I do not have time to play these games. It seems you must simply die.

The darkness caved in on Strov. His body grew cold, the blood freezing in his veins, his mind screaming in sudden, terrifying agony.

The last thought Strov had was hope that Manuel wouldn't blow Strov's entire pension on boar's grog. . . .

ELEVEN

Muzzlecrank used to like being a goblin bruiser. Truly, it had been easy work when he first signed up. Bruisers enforced the peace in Ratchet, and the pay was good. Muzzlecrank's shifts were spent wandering up and down his section of the pier at Ratchet, beating up the occasional drunk or vagabond, taking bribes from shipmasters moving contraband, arresting the ones who were too stupid or too cheap to pay bribes, and generally getting to meet all manner of people.

Muzzlecrank had always thought of himself as a people person. Ratchet was a neutral port—goblins as a rule did not take sides in the numerous conflicts that ravaged the land—and as a result, pretty much every type of creature you were like to find in the world came through at some point or other. Elves, dwarves, humans, orcs, trolls, ogres, even the occasional gnome—it was the crossroads of Kalimdor. Muzzlecrank always liked seeing the different interactions, whether it was dwarves shipping construction materials to elves, elves shipping jewelry to humans, orcs shipping crops to elves, humans shipping fish to ogres, or trolls shipping weapons to pretty much anyone.

Lately, though, things had gotten somewhat less pleasant. Especially between the humans and the orcs—which was problematic insofar as the most common patrons of Ratchet were those two races. Ratchet was right at Durotar's southernmost border, and was the nearest port to Theramore as well.

Just last week, he had had to break up a fight between an orc sailor and a human merchant. The former had apparently stepped on the latter's toe and the human took umbrage. Muzzlecrank had been forced to break them up before the orc beat the human into a pulp, which hadn't been any fun at all. Muzzlecrank preferred to get into fights with vagabonds and drunks because they were kind enough not to fight back. Fighting-mad orcs were another kettle of grease entirely, and Muzzlecrank preferred to stay as far away from them as possible.

Fights like that usually meant that he had to draw his net-gun, and every time he did that he ran the risk of someone figuring out that he was really bad at using the stupid thing. Oh sure, he could fire it easily enough—any idiot could do that; just point and pull the trigger, and a compressed air burst sent a net out to snare whatever you were shooting at—but his aim was lousy, and the net always missed the target and usually made a big mess. Luckily, the site of a bruiser pointing a gun with a giant muzzle at you was enough to stop most fights—or at least slow them down long enough for reinforcements to arrive.

Since then, no more actual fights had broken out, but there were a lot more terse words and heated exchanges happening. It had gotten to the point where many of the merchant ships were now coming into Ratchet with armed escorts—the orc vessels with warriors from Orgrimmar, the human ships with soldiers from Northwatch.

Muzzlecrank's beat was the northernmost section of the pier, a section that had twenty berths. As Muzzlecrank wandered down the wooden-planked pier, he saw that fifteen of the twenty docks were filled, but things were mostly quiet. This was a huge relief. The sun shone down on his face, warming him in his mail armor. Perhaps today would be a good day.

After a few minutes, the sun went away. Muzzlecrank glanced up to see that several clouds had rolled in, and it looked likely to rain soon. Muzzlecrank sighed—he hated rain.

As he neared the end of the dock, he saw a human and an orc having an animated conversation. Muzzlecrank didn't like the look of this. Animated conversations between humans and orcs these days tended to end in violence.

He moved in closer. The human's boat was docked right next to the orc's, in the two northernmost berths.

Muzzlecrank recognized the orc as Captain Klatt of the *Raknor*, a merchant who served as the dealer of crops from the farmers in the Razor Hill region. Though he could not remember the human's name, Muzzlecrank knew his ship was a fishing trawler called the *Passion's Reward* for some odd reason. Muzzlecrank had never understood human naming conventions. Klatt had named the *Raknor* after his brother, who died fighting the Burning Legion, but he hadn't the first clue what the name *Passion's Reward* had to do with anything, least of all fishing.

The exchange was a common one. Farming was difficult in the Dustwallow Marshes where humans had settled on Kalimdor, but there was plenty of fishing. Razor Hill, meanwhile, was too far inland for fishing to be practical—so humans often traded their surplus catches for the orcs' surplus crops.

"I will not trade you my finest salmon for this refuse!"

Muzzlecrank sighed. Obviously today trade was not going to go well.

Klatt stomped his foot. "Refuse? You lyin' little twerp—these are our best crops!"

"A sad commentary on your farming," the human said dryly. "That fruit looks as though it was stepped on by an ogre—smells like it, too."

"I ain't gonna stand here and be insulted by a *human*!"

The human drew himself up to full height, which made him come up to the orc's shoulders. "You're not the one being insulted here. I've brought you my finest catch, and you offer me the bottom of the barrel in exchange."

"Your salmon ain't fit for mulch!"

Too late, Muzzlecrank noticed that the human was armed with what looked like a longsword—while Klatt was weaponless. Assuming the human was skilled in the blade's use, it negated whatever advantage Klatt's size gave him in a fight.

"And your fruit isn't fit for dogs!"

"Coward!"

Muzzlecrank winced at Klatt's words. "Coward" was the biggest insult any orc could deliver.

"Filthy greenskin! I've half a mind to—"

Whatever the human had half a mind to do was lost as Klatt charged him. The human was unable to unsheathe his longsword in time, and the two of them rolled across the dock, Klatt pummeling the human.

Wondering how, precisely, he was supposed to break this up, he was relieved of immediate action by the human's escort. Three guards wearing the plate armor that signified they were part of Lady Proudmoore's forces leapt out of the *Passion's Reward* and pried Klatt off the captain.

However, Klatt would not be dissuaded by a mere three humans. He punched one in the stomach, grabbed the second, and threw him into the third.

Now the orcs were starting to move off the *Raknor* to join in the fray. Muzzlecrank realized he had to do something before this got out of hand.

Hefting his net-gun and hoping with all his heart and

soul that he wouldn't be called upon to use it, he bellowed, "All right, that's it! Cut it out, and I mean *now*, or all'a ya are in deep, unnerstan'?"

Klatt, who was about to jump on the human captain, stopped in his tracks. His target, blood gushing from his nose and mouth, cried, "He attacked me!" The human's voice had an odd twang to it that was probably the result of damage to his nose.

"Yeah, well, you deserved it, goin' back on your word like that," Klatt said with a sneer.

"That's no reason to *kill* a man!"

"I *said*, cut it out!" Muzzlecrank spoke before Klatt could respond. "Both'a ya are under arrest. You either come peaceable-like or in pieces, makes me no never mind." He looked at both the orc warriors and the human soldiers. "This here's goblin country, an' that means I give the orders here, got it? So that gives ya two choices—help me put these two in the hoosegow till an arbiter can take the case, or get your keisters outta Ratchet. Your choice."

Technically, Muzzlecrank's words were true. He had deliberately deepened his voice in the hope that it would give his words an air of authority. But he also knew that he had no way of stopping any of these people if they decided to ignore him and continue fighting. If he shot the net-gun, he'd just get one of the tether posts covered in a net or something.

To his relief, one of the humans said, "We will do as you wish."

Apparently, the orcs weren't about to be seen to be violating the goblins' sovereignty on Ratchet when the humans were, and so one of the orcs quickly said, "So will we."

As he led Klatt and the bleeding human back to the mainland, Muzzlecrank tried to get his breathing under control before he hyperventilated. He wasn't meant for this kind of stress. He wondered what other job he'd be good at. Being a bruiser had *definitely* lost its appeal.

Major Davin was so angry, he started pulling at his beard, and had to consciously force himself to stop. The last time he got that angry, he ripped tufts out, which not only was painful, but violated the dress code.

The focus of his ire was the substance of Corporal Rych's report, given after his hasty return to North-watch from Ratchet. "They actually *arrested* Captain Joq?"

"Well, to be fair, sir," Rych said, "they done arrested that orc, there, too, sir. Soon as the argument het up, one of the goblin's bruisers done stepped in."

"And you *let* them arrest Joq?"

Rych blinked. "I didn't have no choice, sir. Goblins've got jurisdiction in Ratchet. We ain't got no—"

Davin shook his head. "No authority, I know, I know." He got up from his chair and started pacing the office, walking toward the door at first. "It's ridiculous. We shouldn't be subject to this kind of idiocy."

"Sir, I don't see what they'll be—"

"The orcs have a nerve, trying to cheat us like that." He turned and paced toward the window.

Nodding his head quickly, Rych said, "That's certainly true, sir. The fruits they done offered us, why, they was just *vile*, sir. An insult, it was. And then the orc, he done attacked the cap'n. For no reason, neither."

The major stopped pacing when he reached the window. He stared out at the view of the Great Sea. Small waves lapped gently against the sandy beach. It painted a peaceful picture, one that Davin knew was deceptive. "This is out of control. If the orcs keep on like this, it's only a matter of time before we are at war once again."

"I don't think that'll be happenin', sir." Rych sounded skeptical, but Davin knew better.

"Oh, it will, Corporal, of that you can be *absolutely* sure. And with the tauren and the trolls on their side, they will overwhelm us—unless we are prepared." He turned to the door. "Private!"

Private Oreil came in. As always when he saw his aide, Davin sighed. No matter how many times the young private was fitted, his armor was always too big on him. "Yes, sir?"

"Send a message to Theramore right away. We need reinforcements as soon as possible."

"Yes, sir, right away, sir." Oreil saluted and left the watch office to go find the scrying stone that Lady Proudmoore had provided to facilitate communication between Northwatch and Theramore. Detailed conversations couldn't be held through it, but messages could be sent.

Rych scratched his cheek thoughtfully. "Uh, sir, with all due respect, and all—is this bein' such a good idea, sir?"

"Very much so." Davin sat back down at his desk, no longer feeling the need to rip out his beard hairs now that he was taking action. "I'm not letting those green-skinned bastards catch us off guard."

TWELVE

A egwynn really wished the annoying young
woman would just go away.

That wasn't going to happen, of course. Aegwynn was too much of a realist to think otherwise. But
it didn't stop her from wishing it with all her heart. She
had been alone for two decades and had come to appreciate being by herself. Indeed, she'd been happier these
past twenty years than the hundreds of years prior to
her exile to Kalimdor.

She had truly hoped that these highlands, surrounded
as they were by impassable mountains, were remote
enough, and that the wards were low-level enough, that
no one would find her. In retrospect, that was a forlorn
hope.

"I can't believe you're still alive."

This Proudmoore woman sounded like a teenager.
Aegwynn knew it wasn't her standard mode only be-

cause she had modulated into it upon learning who Aegwynn was.

Proudmoore went on: "You've always been one of my heroes. When I was an apprentice, I studied the records of your deeds—you were the greatest of the Guardians."

Shuddering at the thought of what those doddering old fools at the Violet Citadel would have written about her, Aegwynn said, "Hardly." Unable to stand this anymore, she lifted the bucket of water and headed back to the hut. If she was lucky, Proudmoore would leave her be.

But Aegwynn wasn't particularly lucky today.

Proudmoore followed her. "It was because of you that I was able to become a wizard."

"Reason enough for me to be sorry I became one," Aegwynn muttered.

"I don't understand—why are you here? Why haven't you told anyone you're still alive? Honestly, we could've used your help against the Burning—"

Dropping the bucket to the ground, Aegwynn whirled on Proudmoore. "I am here for my own reasons, and they are not yours to know. Now leave me in peace!"

Unfortunately, all this served to do was cause Proudmoore to drop the teenager affect and go back to being the leader she apparently was. "I'm afraid I can't do that, Magna. You're too important to—"

"I'm not important to *anything*! Don't you understand, you *stupid* little girl? I'm not fit for human company—or orc company, troll company, dwarf company, you name it."

That got the infant's back up. Aegwynn could see the magic roiling within her and realized that, child though she may be, she was quite powerful. She had gotten through the wards without Aegwynn's even noticing, after all, and that bespoke a certain skill. "I'm not a 'little girl.' I'm a wizard of the Kirin Tor."

"And I'm a thousand years old, so as far as I'm concerned, you've got a few centuries to go before I might consider calling you something other than a little girl, little girl. Now go away—I just want to be left alone."

"Why?" Proudmoore sounded genuinely confused, which led Aegwynn to think that the young wizard hadn't really read her history—or it had been thoroughly bowdlerized by the time Proudmoore got to it. The girl continued: "You were the one who blazed the trail for women to *become* wizards. You're one of the unsung heroes of Azeroth. How can you turn your back—"

"Like this." Aegwynn turned and walked into the house, abandoning the bucket. She'd get it later.

Naturally, Proudmoore didn't give up, but followed her through the rickety wooden door. "Magna, you're—"

Now standing in what she jokingly called the sitting room—it was the only room in the hut, so it served as bedroom, kitchen, and dining room as well—she cried, "Stop *calling* me that! I'm not a mage anymore, I'm not a hero at *all,* and I don't want you in my house. You say that I blazed the trail for women to become mages—if anything, I'm the best reason why women should *never* become mages."

"You're wrong," Proudmoore said. "It's because of you—"

Putting her hands to her ears, Aegwynn said, "For the love of all that is holy in this world, will you please *stop* that?"

Quietly, Proudmoore said, "I'm not saying anything you shouldn't already be aware of. If not for your work, the demons would have come much sooner, and we—"

"And what difference did *that* make, exactly?" Aegwynn sneered at the girl. "The demons still came, and Lordaeron was still destroyed, the Lich King still reigns, and Sargeras still won."

Proudmoore winced at the mention of the Lich King for some reason, but Aegwynn didn't really care enough to inquire why. Then the girl said, "You can deny your accomplishments all you wish, but it changes nothing. You were an inspiration to all—" She smiled. "—to all the little girls who wanted to grow up to become mages. At the citadel, my favorite story was always the one about how you were chosen to be the first female Guardian by Scavell, who was the first mage to see the value of a female apprentice, and how the Guardians of Tirisfal applauded the choice and—"

Aegwynn couldn't help it. She laughed. She laughed long and she laughed hard. In fact, she was having trouble breathing, she was laughing so hard. She started coughing, but managed to get it under control after a moment. Her body was finally, after a millennium, starting to age and break down, but she still had some vitality left, and she wouldn't be rendered helpless by a fit of laughter.

It was, however, the best laugh she'd had in centuries.

Proudmoore looked like someone had fed her a lemon, her face was so sour. "I fail to see what's so amusing."

"Of course not." Aegwynn chuckled, and took a few deep breaths. "If you believe that garbage, you wouldn't." A final breath, which turned into a sigh. "Since you insist on invading my privacy, Lady Jaina Proudmoore of the oh-so-noble city of Theramore, then have a seat." She indicated the straw chair that she had spent the third year of her exile in this place putting together, but then refused to ever sit in. "I will tell you the real story of how I became a Guardian of Tirisfal, and why I am the last person you should consider to be any kind of hero . . ."

Eight hundred and forty-seven years ago . . .

For the first time in years, the Tirisfal Glades frightened Aegwynn. The forests that lay just north of the capital of Lordaeron had always been a place of beauty and of quiet, away from the hustle and the bustle. Her mother had first taken her here on a camping trip when she was a girl. Little Aegwynn had found it to be frightening and fascinating all at the same time. She had been

Warcraft: The Sunwell Trilogy brings you the world of Azeroth as you've never seen it before: as a graphic novel! The three-volume series follows the adventures of Kalecgos, a blue dragon who seeks the mystically powerful Sunwell, and Anveena, a maiden with a mysterious secret.

What starts as a fight for survival turns into a quest to save the entire High Elven Kingdom from the forces of the Undead Scourge.

Written by Richard A. Knaak
Illustrated by Jae-Hwan Kim
Lettering and Layout by
Rob Steen and James Dashiell

Published by
🔮 TOKYOPOP®

Volume 1: "Dragonhunt" on sale now.
Volume 2: "Shadows of Ice" on sale March 2006.
Check the manga or graphic novel section of your favorite bookseller.

HE HAD WITH HIM THE ORB OF NER'ZHUL...

...AND HAD COME IN SEARCH OF SOMETHING UPON WHICH TO USE ITS ACCURSED ABILITIES.

surprised at the animals ranging freely, stunned by the incredible colors of the vegetation, and amazed at how many stars she could see in the night sky away from the torchlight and lanterns of the city.

Over time, the fear fell away, replaced by joy and wonder and, at times, relief.

Until today. Today the fear was back in full force.

She had been apprentice to the wizard Scavell since before puberty, working alongside four others—all boys, of course. Aegwynn had always wanted to be a mage but had been told repeatedly by her parents that she would grow up to become someone's wife, and that was all there was to it, and her dallying about with herbs and such was fine for now, but soon she'd need to learn more important skills, like sewing and cooking. . . .

This assurance lasted right up until she met Scavell, and he invited her to become an apprentice—making it clear that he wouldn't accept no for an answer. Her parents both wept openly that they were losing their little girl, but Aegwynn was thrilled. She was studying to become a mage!

Back then, there were only three other apprentices—Falric, Jonas, and Manfred, who were as irritating as every other boy Aegwynn had known, but a little more tolerable. The fourth, Natale, came a year later.

Today, Scavell announced that he was a member of a secret order known as the Guardians of Tirisfal. Aegwynn's first thought was that the forest she loved was named after them, but it turned out to be the other way around—they called themselves that because they met in those glades, and had for many centuries. This surprised Aegwynn, as she had never seen any of these meetings, despite making regular trips to the glades for years.

Then Scavell said they were going to the glades to meet the *Tirisfalen*.

The boys went on about secret societies and how amazing that was, like it was some kind of adventure, but Aegwynn didn't participate. She wanted to know *what* exactly this *Tirisfalen* was—Scavell was vague on the subject. Where the boys were content to trust Scavell's word, Aegwynn wanted to know more.

"You'll see soon enough, my girl," Scavell had said in response to her question. He always called her "my girl."

When Scavell brought them out to the glade, Aegwynn was confused, for there was no one in the clearing they stood in.

Then, moments later, just as she was about to ask Scavell what was going on, there was a flash of light and she found herself, Scavell, and her fellow apprentices surrounded by seven people standing in a perfect circle around them. Three of them were human, three were elves, and one was a gnome. All of them were male.

"We have chosen," one of the elves said.

Falric asked, "Chosen what?"

The gnome said, "Be silent, boy, you'll find out soon enough."

Turning to Scavell, the elf said, "You have trained all five of your students well, Magna Scavell."

Aegwynn frowned; she'd never heard that honorific before.

"However, there is one student that has stood out from the others. One student who has proven inquisitive in the ways of magic beyond ordinary curiosity, who has shown aptitude for spellcasting that is unparalleled, and who has already mastered the Meitre scrolls."

Now Aegwynn's heart raced. The night elf Meitre was a great wizard from many thousands of years ago. Elven mages didn't attempt to cast from Meitre's scrolls until the final year of their apprenticeships, and human mages often didn't even try until after that apprenticeship was completed. Aegwynn, however, was casting Meitre's spells at will by the end of her first year.

She had also been doing so in secret—Scavell insisted that it would "annoy the boys."

Falric looked at his fellow apprentices in turn. "Who was casting Meitre's spells?"

Grinning, Aegwynn said triumphantly, "*I* was."

"Who said you could do *that*?" Manfred asked angrily.

Speaking in his papery voice, Scavell said, "*I* did, young Manfred. And you and Falric would be wise not to speak out of turn again."

Bowing their heads, Falric and Manfred both said, "Yes, sir."

The elf went on: "What you must now be told, all of

you, is that there is a war being fought. It is not known to the general populace, only to the community of wizards, of which all of you will some day soon be a part. Demons have invaded our world, and they grow more aggressive with each passing year, despite our best efforts to stymie them."

"Indeed," the gnome put in, earning him a mild glare from the elf, "likely *because* of those efforts, which serve only to anger them."

"Demons?" Natale sounded scared. He'd always had a fear of demons.

"Yes," one of the humans said. "At every turn, they try to destroy us. Only the wizards can stand against them."

"The *Tirisfalen*," the elf added, with a glance at the human that indicated that he didn't appreciate *this* interruption, either, "have been charged with protecting this world from demonkind, and we have created a Guardian. The finest young mages in the land are brought together by the current Guardian—your master Scavell, in this case—who trains them. We then determine which is the most qualified to become the new Guardian."

"The choice wasn't easy," the gnome said.

Jonas muttered, "It be a stupid choice."

"What did you say, young man?" another elf asked.

"I said the choice be stupid. Aegwynn's a *girl*. She be fit for a wise-woman, givin' out herbal remedies to the villagers or summat, but that be all! We all of us be *mages*!"

Aegwynn looked in shock and disgust at Jonas. She had grown rather fond of Jonas, and the two of them had slept together a couple of times. They had kept their liaison secret from the other apprentices, though Scavell knew about it—there was nothing that escaped the old mage's gaze. The last thing she had expected were those words from his lips—Falric's, maybe, he was a pompous ass, but not Jonas—and Aegwynn swore to herself that Jonas would never get her in bed again. . . .

"It is true," an older human said with a sigh, "that women are emotional and prone to excessive displays that are unbecoming of a mage. But it is also true that Aegwynn has the most potential of any of the youths that Scavell has found, and we cannot afford for the Guardian to be anything less than the best—even if that means giving the position to a girl."

At that, Aegwynn bristled. "With respect, good sirs, I will be as good a mage as any of these boys. In fact, I think I will be better—because I had to overcome so much more to get here."

The elf chuckled. "She raises a fine point."

"So, waitasec," Natale said, "you mean that she's gonna be this, uh, whadayacall, Guardian thing, and we get, what, nothin'?"

"Not at all," the elf said. "You will each have important roles to play. All the wizards of our order are fighting this battle. It is simply that the Guardian's role is the *most* important."

Turning to her mentor, Aegwynn asked, "Scavell—

what of you? Why are you giving up being Guardian?"

Scavell smiled. "I am old, my girl, and very tired. Fighting the hordes of demonkind is a game for the young. I wish to live out my few remaining years preparing the next generation." He turned to the boys. "Rest assured, I will continue to be your mentor."

"Swell," Falric muttered. All four boys were sulking.

"If anything," the gnome said testily, "the fact that you're being so immature about this is precisely why we chose Aegwynn over you."

"Besides," the older human added, "the Guardian must be the vessel of the council. I suspect that a girl will be less willful and will understand the chain of command, as it were."

"This isn't a military engagement," one of the other humans said.

Aegwynn couldn't help herself. "You described this as a war."

"Quite right," the elf said with a small chuckle. Then he looked right at Aegwynn with eyes that seemed to bore into her very soul. "You still have some preparations to undergo, girl, before you must undergo the transfer of power. The magic of all the *Tirisfalen* will be granted to you. Understand this, Aegwynn—you are taking on the gravest responsibility any mage can accept."

"I understand," Aegwynn said, though she wasn't entirely sure she did. But she wanted to be a mage more than anything else, and she knew that the primary responsibility of any wizard was to keep the world safe. At its best, magic was used by wizards to bring order to a chaotic world, and Aegwynn knew that that would be a lot of work.

She just hadn't realized how much work. Or what Scavell's real motives for showing her Meitre's scrolls were.

Falric stepped forward. "Dammit, I'm as good as any girl! Better, even! I can even cast one of Meitre's spells! Watch!" Falric closed his eyes, then opened them again and stared at a rock that was jutting up from the ground right in front of where the elf stood. He muttered an incantation, then repeated it—Meitre's spells all required double incantations, which Scavell had said was a security precaution.

A flash of light, and then the rock glowed faintly with a yellowish hue. Falric sneered at Aegwynn, and then grinned at the mages that surrounded them.

"Rock to gold," the gnome said. "How unoriginal."

"Actually," the elf said with a smile, "it is fool's gold."

Falric's grin fell. "What? It can't be!" He cast a quick identification spell, and then his face fell even farther. "Dammit!"

"You have a great deal to learn," the elf said, "but you have much potential, all of you. Falric, Manfred, Jonas, Natale, you will find that potential as Scavell's students." Again the soul-boring gaze. "Aegwynn, your destiny will come quite a bit sooner. We will reconvene in this glade in a month's time for the transfer of power. There is much you have to prepare for."

With that, all the councillors disappeared in a flash of light.

A month later, having taught Aegwynn about the legions of demons and their horrific minions that had been trying—and, through the grace of Guardians like Scavell, failing—to encroach upon the world, Scavell passed on the power of the Guardian to Aegwynn. It was like nothing she'd ever experienced before. Spells that once took all her concentration now required only the briefest of thoughts. Her perceptions changed as well, as she saw far beneath the surface of everything. Where it once took an effort—or a complex spell—to determine the nature of a plant or the emotional state of an animal, she could now divine it at the merest glance.

A year after that, Scavell died quietly in his sleep. When he realized he was dying, he had arranged to find new mages for Jonas, Natale, and Manfred to study under. Falric, at that point, was ready to be out on his own. Scavell willed all his belongings, as well as his servants, to Aegwynn.

Less than a month after Scavell's death, Aegwynn returned from the small village of Jortas in time to receive a mystical summons from the council.

As soon as she arrived at Tirisfal Glade, the gnome—whose name, she had since learned, was Erbag—said, "What do you think you were doing in Jortas?"

"Saving them from Zmodlor." Aegwynn would have thought that her answer was self-evident.

"And did you think to learn more about Zmodlor before you destroyed him? Did you plan a strategy that would dispose of him in a manner that would contain him without the populace of Jortas learning the truth? Or did you just blindly charge in and flail about, hoping you might succeed?"

Fatigue and irritation combined to make Aegwynn a bit more forthright than she truly should have been with the council. "None of those, Erbag, as you well know. There was no time to plan such a strategy or learn more. Doing so would have endangered the children in the schoolhouse that Zmodlor had taken possession of. There were *children* in there. Was I to hang back and—"

"What you were to *do*," Erbag said, "was as you were told. Did Scavell not teach you in the ways of the *Tirisfalen*? We proceed with caution and with—"

Aegwynn interrupted the gnome right back. "What you *do*, Erbag, is react. And that's *all* you do, and it's why you've made so little headway against these foul creatures over the last several centuries. Zmodlor was able to take over an entire schoolhouse and was prepared to use the children of Jortas for a ritual that would have poisoned their souls. It was only purest chance that I detected the foul stench of demon-magic and was able to arrive in time. Your methods are reactive."

"Of *course* they are!" Erbag was waving his arms back and forth now. "This council was created to *react* to the threat of the—"

"And it hasn't *worked*. If we are truly to stand firm against these monsters who would invade and destroy our homes, we cannot allow them to encroach upon us so easily that they capture *children* before we even know they're here. We must be *proactive* in seeking them out and eliminating them, or we *will* be overrun."

Erbag was not convinced. "And when the people start to realize that their lives are in danger and they panic uncontrollably?"

Rather than reply to the question, Aegwynn looked at the other councillors. "Does Erbag speak for you all, or is he simply the loudest?"

The oldest of the elves on the council, Relfthra, favored Aegwynn with a small smile. "Both, in fact, Magna." The smile fell. "Erbag is correct in that you are too reckless. Zmodlor was a minor demon in the service of Sargeras; he might have been able to provide us with useful intelligence about his master."

"Yes, and he *might* have killed all those children before providing us with that intelligence."

"Perhaps. But that is a risk that sometimes we must take in order to fight this war."

Aegwynn was aghast. "We're talking about the lives of *children*. Besides which, this isn't a war, it's a holding action—at best. And it will get us all killed, child and adult alike, if we're not careful." Before any of the other mages could criticize her, she said, "August mages of the council, with all respect, I beg you—I am exhausted and wish to sleep. Is there anything else?"

Relfthra's face darkened. "Remember your place, Magna Aegwynn. You are the Guardian, but you serve that function as the arm of the Council of Tirisfal. Never forget that."

"I doubt that you will ever allow me to," Aegwynn muttered. "If that is all?"

"For now," Relfthra said. The words were barely out of his mouth when Aegwynn teleported back to the Violet Citadel, in desperate need of sleep.

THIRTEEN

Lorena was disappointed, but not entirely surprised, to see Kristoff seated on Lady Proudmoore's throne. The lady herself avoided sitting on the thing whenever possible, but the chamberlain would insist on using it when he was left in charge.

Kristoff wasn't so much sitting in the throne as draping himself on it. His thin shoulders were slumped, and he was seated at an angle, one leg hanging off the side. He was reading a scroll when Lorena came in, led by Duree. "Colonel Lorena to see you, sir," the old woman said meekly.

"What is it, Colonel?" Kristoff asked without looking up from the scroll.

"Private Strov has disappeared," she said without preamble.

Now he looked up from the scroll, an eyebrow raised. "Is that name supposed to mean something to me?"

"It is if you bothered to pay attention to meetings in the lady's chambers."

Setting the scroll aside, Kristoff straightened in the throne. "Modify your tone when speaking to me in this room, Colonel."

Lorena looked aghast at the chamberlain. "I'll speak to you how I please in whatever room we're standing in, thank you very much. Lady Proudmoore asked you to manage Theramore in her absence. That doesn't mean you get to *be* the lady." She smirked. "You haven't the equipment for it, for starters."

Kristoff's eyebrows tented into a frown. "Until Lady Proudmoore returns, I am empowered to act in her stead, and you will treat that office with respect."

"Your office is that of chamberlain, Kristoff, which entitles you to be an advisor to Lady Proudmoore, same as me. So don't go getting delusions of grandeur."

Leaning back in the throne and picking the scroll back up, Kristoff asked in a bored voice, "You came in here for a reason?"

"As I said, Private Strov has disappeared. He's the one I sent to investigate the Burning Blade. I've talked to his brother—Manuel says they arranged everything in the Demonsbane. Strov sat in a corner, Manuel talked to the person they thought was with the Burning Blade, and Strov followed him. That was the night before last, and I haven't heard a thing since."

"And why is this my concern?" Kristoff still sounded bored.

"Because, you gibbering imbecile, he was investigating this Burning Blade. The same Burning Blade that attacked me and my people in Northwatch. I think it's suspicious, don't you?"

"Not particularly." He set the scroll down again. "People desert the military all the time. It's a sad reality—one that I would think you'd be aware of, Colonel."

Tightly, Lorena said, "I *am* aware of it, Chamberlain, but I also know Strov. He'd sooner hack off a limb than desert. He's the best soldier I've got. I want to tear the island apart and *find* him."

"No."

Lorena's hand went to her sword hilt instinctively, but she knew it would be foolish to stab the man sitting on Theramore's throne, however much he didn't deserve the seat and did deserve the stabbing. "What do you mean 'no'?"

"I assume the colonel is familiar with the definition of the word. . . ."

"Very funny." She took her hand away from the sword hilt and walked over to the room's large window, as much so she wouldn't have to look at Kristoff as anything. The skies were so clear that she could see Alcaz Island to the northeast. "This Burning Blade has me concerned, Chamberlain. They have use of magic, and they—"

"Right now, Colonel, the Burning Blade is little more than a rumor—one, I might add, that you cannot substantiate, since your private has gone missing. I'm afraid I cannot devote Theramore's resources to finding a deserter—not when those resources are needed elsewhere."

Whirling around, Lorena asked, "What are you talking about?"

"Your arrival has saved me the trouble of summoning you," Kristoff said.

Lorena had to wonder why he didn't bring this up in the first place, and said so.

Sneering, Kristoff said, "It is not your place to question the person who sits on this throne, Colonel, merely to obey that person's orders. Right now, that person is telling you that I have just received word that orc troops are massing at Kolkar Crag. That's the nearest portion of Durotar to Northwatch."

Not bothering to point out that she knew damn well what Kolkar Crag's location was, she asked with a frown, "When did this happen?"

"Just this morning. Major Davin needs additional reinforcements, and I want you to lead them."

While Lorena's job description did not include supervision of all troop movements within Theramore and Northwatch, it did include her being apprised of them. "*Additional* reinforcements? When was Northwatch reinforced?"

"Yesterday. There have been several incidents along the Merchant Coast, involving orcs provoking humans. Some have even led to arrests—right now a human captain is being held in Ratchet because an orc attacked him."

Lorena nodded, having seen that particular report. "What of it? The goblins have the right to stop brawls."

"This wasn't a brawl!" Kristoff was shouting now, a state of affairs that surprised Lorena. The chamberlain was often supercilious, condescending, arrogant—and, she was occasionally willing to admit, brilliant and very good at his job—but she'd never heard the thin man raise his voice before.

"Whether or not it was a brawl," she said in a quiet tone deliberately chosen to belie Kristoff's increasing volume, "is not the point. Why was Northwatch being fortified?"

"I told you, orc troops—"

"I mean the initial reinforcement."

Kristoff shrugged. "Major Davin thought it necessary, and I agreed."

Lorena shook her head and turned back to the window. "Major Davin doesn't think the orcs are worth the time of day, Chamberlain. I wouldn't trust his statements on the subject. He's probably exaggerating."

"I don't believe he is—certainly not now with troops massing." Kristoff got up and stepped down off the throne, walking to stand alongside Lorena. "Colonel, if Northwatch is to be the front of another war between humans and orcs, we need to be ready. That's why I sent the two garrisons, as well as the Elite Guard."

At that, Lorena's jaw fell open. Shifting her position

both so she was facing Kristoff and also so she was a bit farther away from him, she said, "The Elite Guard? Their function is to guard Lady Proudmoore."

Calmly, Kristoff said, "Who is presently out of contact and can take care of herself. Better they be used at Northwatch than be allowed to sit uselessly here."

Again, Lorena shook her head. "You're making an incredible leap, Kristoff. Right now, we've got a few tense situations. That doesn't mean another war."

"Perhaps not—but I'd rather be prepared for one we don't have to fight than not be prepared for one we have to."

The logic was sound, but Lorena still didn't like it. "And what if the orcs interpret this as a hostile act?"

"It's how I am choosing to interpret *their* actions, Colonel. Either way, we need our best troop commander on-site. That is why I want you to lead the regiment that reinforces Northwatch. Speed is of the essence, so you may take your senior staff on the airship to set things up—the rest of the troops will travel by boat, arriving in time for you to give them their assignments when they catch up to you."

Lorena sighed. If the airship was already prepared, Kristoff had made this decision before she ever walked in the room. Still, she had one last card to play. "I think we should wait until Lady Proudmoore returns."

"You're entitled to think that." Kristoff walked back over to the throne and sat in it, placing his arms rather theatrically on the flared rests on either side of him.

"However, Lady Proudmoore is busy helping her precious orc friends, while they mount defenses and prepare to destroy us. I will not allow what she has built to be destroyed by her own shortsightedness when it comes to Thrall. Now then, Colonel, you have your orders. Kindly carry them out."

"Kristoff, this is a mistake. Let me try to find Strov and find out—"

"No." Then Kristoff softened, and lowered his arms to his side. "Very well, Colonel, I will grant you one concession: you may assign two soldiers to search for Private Strov. I can spare no more than that."

She supposed that was the best she was going to get from the chamberlain. "Thank you. Now if you'll excuse me, it seems I have to put a senior staff together."

Picking up the scroll once again with his right hand, Kristoff waved dismissively with his left. "You may go."

She turned on her heel and angrily left the throne room.

FOURTEEN

As Aegwynn told the story of how she was made Guardian, Jaina found surprise piling upon shock. The histories she had read had always painted the appointment of Aegwynn in nothing but a positive light. The notion that the council was reluctant to appoint her, and did so despite misgivings about her sex—and that they would have resisted her methods so thoroughly—was completely alien to her.

Of course, Aegwynn's memories of those days were several centuries old. "Your account of matters does not match what is in the history scrolls, Magna."

"No," Aegwynn said with a sigh. "It wouldn't. Better to let you young mages think that all wizards function in perfect harmony. Figure you might learn from their lack of example." She shook her head and slumped a bit farther in her seat. "But no, they didn't want a girl there, and only appointed me because they didn't have a choice. I *was* the best qualified—certainly more than the other four. And they regretted it every minute." She sat back up straight. "In the end, we all did. If it wasn't for me . . ."

Jaina shook her head. "That's ridiculous. You did so much."

"What did I do? I insisted that Tirisfal be more proactive in dealing with the demons, but what did my insistence accomplish, exactly? For eight centuries, I tried to stem the tide, to no avail. Zmodlor was just the first. So many demons, so many battles, and in the end I was still tricked by Sargeras. I—"

This time, Jaina didn't need to hear the story. "I know what happened to you when you faced Sargeras. You destroyed his physical form, but his soul remained inside you—and was passed on to Medivh."

Chuckling bitterly, Aegwynn said, "And you still think I was a great wizard? I let my arrogance interfere with my judgment. I assumed the *Tirisfalen* to be a group of hidebound old fools, rather than what they truly were: experienced mages who knew better than me. After I 'defeated' Sargeras, I became *more* arrogant, if that's even possible. I ignored every summons the council sent me, disregarded their procedures, disobeyed their orders. After all, I beat Sargeras, and he was a *god,* so what did *they* know?" She snarled. "I was *such* an idiot."

"Don't be ridiculous." Jaina couldn't believe this. Bad enough that the greatest wizard of her time, the woman she'd idolized all her life, turned out to be such an unpleasant person, but now she was just being idiotic. "It was *Sargeras*. Any mage would have made the same mistake you did. As you said, he was a god. He knew he would have to trick you because of your power, and he knew how to manipulate you. What you did was perfectly natural."

Aegwynn stared at one of the corners of the ramshackle hut that she apparently called home. "I did far far more than that. There was also Medivh."

Now Jaina was even more confused. "I knew Medivh, Magna. He was—"

Whirling to look at Jaina, Aegwynn snapped, "I'm not talking about *what* my son was. I'm talking about *how* he was."

"What do you mean?" Jaina asked, genuinely confused. "Medivh was fathered by Nielas Aran, and—"

" 'Fathered'?" Aegwynn let out a noise that sounded like a rock shattering. "That's far too generous a term for it."

Sixty-nine years ago . . .

The summons had been insistent this time, which was the only reason why Aegwynn responded to it. The Guardians of Tirisfal had changed over the years. The three elves were the same, but the humans and the gnome had all died and been replaced, and then their replacements died and themselves had successors. In many ways, though, they had not changed at all. Rather than deal with them in any way, or deal with an apprentice, Aegwynn had used her magicks to extend her life so she could continue to do her duty as Guardian.

She had almost fallen to her death while standing on a parapet in Lordaeron, casting a seeker spell for one of Sargeras's former thralls, rumored to be out and about in the city. In the midst of the incantation, the council had decided to hit her with a summons so powerful that she almost lost her balance. It was the third summons in as many days, and the first that had interfered with her ability to function.

Realizing that she would not hear the end of it until she answered, she teleported to the Tirisfal Glade. She stood on top of the very rock Falric—who had also long since died, as had her other three fellow apprentices, all perishing while fighting demons—had transmuted into fool's gold all those centuries ago, time having exposed and tarnished it so it was a dull brown instead of the bright golden color it was eight hundred years past.

"What *is* it that's so important that you interrupt my work?"

"It has been eight centuries, Aegwynn," one of the new humans said. Aegwynn had never bothered to learn his name. "It is past time you relinquished your duties."

Drawing herself up to her full height—which made her taller than any of the men surrounding her in this glade—she said, "I am properly addressed as 'Magna.' That's one of those ridiculous rules you insist on foisting upon the magical world." The word was a dwarven one meaning "protector," and had been the honorific for every Guardian since the first. Aegwynn didn't care much for titles, but the council's insistence on the rules and regulations, and their disapproval of her flaunting them, made her sensitive to their own violations.

Relfthra threw it back in her face. "Ah, so *now* you're a stickler for rules, eh?"

The human gave Relfthra a look, and then said, "The *point*, Magna, is that you know as well as any of us the risks of what you are doing. The longer you extend your age, the greater the risk that it will be undone. The de-aging magicks are not precise, nor are they stable. In mid-conflict, in mid-casting, you could find yourself suddenly brought to your natural age. If that happens without a successor—"

Aegwynn held up a hand. The last thing she needed from these fools was a lecture on the ways of magic. She was a stronger magician than any of them. Had they faced down Sargeras himself? "Very well. I will find a successor and transfer the Guardian power to that person."

Gritting his teeth, the human said, "*We* will choose your successor, just as we chose Scavell's—and that of every Guardian before him."

"No. I shall make the choice. I believe I know better than anyone what is involved in being a Guardian— certainly more than you who stand around this glade and make pronouncements while the rest of us do the actual work."

"Magna—" the human started, but Aegwynn wished to hear no more.

"I have heard your advice, and for once it is worth heeding." She smiled. "I suppose it was bound to happen eventually. Even a village idiot may stumble upon a valuable philosophy once in a while. When my successor is chosen, you will be informed. That is all."

Without waiting to be dismissed, she teleported back to the parapet. While the council's words were in fact true, she *was* in the midst of doing her duty. She once again cast the seeker spell to determine if the demon was loose in Lordaeron, as rumored.

Once that was taken care of—there was no demon, only some teenagers indulging in magicks they didn't understand; had they continued, that demon would have been summoned, but Aegwynn was able to forestall their adolescent efforts—she traveled to Stormwind, specifically to the home of Nielas Aran.

Aran had been an admirer of hers for many years. Aegwynn barely paid any attention to him, except insofar as he was more talented than most of the mages who were part of the *Tirisfalen*. He was blissfully free of the prejudices of the council, and had done well by his craft, serving also as the court magician for King Landan Wrynn. Were she several centuries younger, she might have admired his steel blue eyes and his broad shoulders and his easy laugh.

However, she wasn't several centuries younger, and so had neither interest in him nor desire to even acknowledge his interest in her. She'd had plenty of dalliances in her younger days, starting with Jonas, but she'd long since lost patience with them. Eight hundred years of life had exposed romance to be a mass of fallacy and artifice, and she had neither the time nor the inclination for it.

Still and all, she managed to dredge up the flirtatiousness that she had first used on Jonas as a teenager, and started speaking to Aran. She suddenly became fascinated in his hobbies and his interest in dwarven music.

All of it served one purpose, which was for him to share his bed with her.

The next morning, she knew that she had been impregnated by his seed. She had been mildly disheartened to realize that the embryo within her would grow to be a male child. She had been hoping for a daughter, as yet another poke in the eye to the Guardians of Tirisfal. But even so, this boy would serve the purpose for which he had been conceived.

Taking her leave of a rather disappointed Aran—who truly had expected little else, but had been hoping that Aegwynn could at least have been polite about it—she departed Stormwind. For nine months, she performed her tasks as Guardian as much as she could, and eventually bore Medivh. Only then did she return, handing the infant to Aran and declaring him to be her heir.

"I can see by the look on your face that you're horrified." Aegwynn said the words to Jaina with a vicious smile.

"I am." Jaina spoke true. She had fought alongside

Medivh—it was he who had encouraged Jaina to ally herself with Thrall and the orcs against the Burning Legion—but she'd had no idea that the prophet's origins were so tawdry. Indeed, she knew very little about him, save that he had returned from the dead and was trying to atone for his sins by doing everything he could to stop the Burning Legion.

"That is why I told you the story," Aegwynn said. "I'm no hero, I'm no role model, I'm no shining beacon to inspire wizards of any sex. What I am is an arrogant ass who let her power and the wiles of a clever demon destroy her—and the rest of the world."

Jaina shook her head. She remembered many conversations with Kristoff about how the lessons of history are rarely in the written word, for such accounts were invariably biased in favor of what the writer wished the reader to know about. She realized that the histories she'd read about the Guardians of Tirisfal in Antonidas's library were as vulnerable to such biases as the historical texts that Kristoff had spoken of.

Then, suddenly, a feeling pricked at the back of Jaina's neck. She stood up.

So did Aegwynn—no doubt the old woman felt the same thing. She confirmed it by saying, "The wards are back up."

Jaina found it interesting that Aegwynn felt that—especially given Jaina's own ability to break down the wards without her knowledge. It confirmed a growing suspicion of hers.

Of greater concern, however, was that these wards felt far more powerful. And had entirely the wrong feel. "Something is wrong."

"Yes—I know this magic. Never thought I'd encounter it again, to be honest." Aegwynn made a *tch* noise. "In fact, I'm not really sure how it's possible."

Before asking Aegwynn to explain herself, Jaina had to make sure she could penetrate the wards. She attempted a teleport spell, this time adding a ward-penetration incantation to the mix, bracing herself for the ensuing pain should it not succeed.

Sure enough, it didn't. It would have worked previously—she hadn't used the penetration spell to teleport the thunder lizards only because she needed to investigate the highlands before bringing hundreds of agitated animals there. Closing her eyes briefly to block out the pain, she turned to Aegwynn. "I can't get through them."

"I was afraid of that." Aegwynn sighed, apparently not relishing being stuck with the "little girl."

Jaina wasn't entirely thrilled with the prospect, either, but more because she couldn't fulfill her promise to Thrall while trapped in these highlands.

"You said you knew this magic?"

Aegwynn nodded. "Yes. Remember Zmodlor, the first demon I encountered—the one who imprisoned those schoolchildren?"

Jaina nodded.

"These wards are his."

FIFTEEN

Kristoff hated sitting on the throne.

Intellectually, he understood the need for it. Leaders needed to convey that they were in a position of authority, and the intimidating physicality of a giant chair that was raised above everyone else in the room conveyed that authority beautifully.

But he hated sitting in it. He was convinced that he would damage the authority of the position by making some kind of mistake. Because Kristoff knew his limitations—he was no leader. He'd spent years observing leaders firsthand and studying leaders he didn't have access to, and knew as much as anyone living about what good leaders had to do right and what bad leaders often did wrong. One thing he had learned early on was that the arrogant rarely lasted long. Leaders made mistakes, and the arrogant never admitted to such a thing, a conflict that often resulted in self-destruction—or destruction from outside forces. Certainly, that was true of

Kristoff's previous employer, Garithos; if the Highlord had simply listened to Kristoff—or any of the other six people giving him the same advice—he wouldn't have sided with the Forsaken. As Kristoff had predicted, the undead creatures betrayed Garithos and his warriors and led to his downfall. By that time, Kristoff had left for greener pastures.

This tendency was rather unfortunate, because the arrogant were usually the only ones who pursued leadership positions in the first place. The conundrum had fascinated Kristoff as a young student, and also explained why there were so few truly great leaders.

Kristoff was also self-aware enough to know that he was *incredibly* arrogant. That supreme confidence in his own abilities was why he made such a good advisor to Lady Proudmoore, but it was also why he was so terribly unfit to take her place.

Nevertheless, he did as he was told, and served in the lady's stead until she returned from her ridiculous errand.

On top of everything else, Kristoff also hated the throne because it was a damned uncomfortable piece of furniture. For the proper effect, one had to sit on it straight, with arms on the armrests, gazing down upon one's petitioners with an all-knowing eye. The problem was, sitting like that was hell on Kristoff's back. He could only avoid spine-chewing agony if he sat slumped, and off to the side. The problem there was that he looked like he was treating the throne like a sofa, which was not the right impression to give.

It was a difficult situation, and Kristoff fervently wished that the lady hadn't hared off into orc country to do whatever ludicrous thing she was doing. As if the needs of Theramore weren't of considerably more import than the disposition of some rampaging reptiles in Durotar.

Lady Proudmoore had done amazing things. For starters, few of her sex had been able to accomplish what she had done, either as a wizard or as a ruler. Oh, there were plenty of female monarchs, true, but they generally came to their position by heredity or marriage, not through sheer force of will as the lady had done. While it was Medivh who first encouraged the notion, it was Jaina Proudmoore who managed the heretofore inconceivable task of uniting human and orc. She was, in his expert opinion, the greatest leader the world had ever seen, and Kristoff considered it an honor to be her most trusted advisor.

Which was why her blind spot for the orcs was so maddening. Kristoff could understand it—of all the leaders he had encountered and studied, the only one he might consider Lady Proudmoore's equal was Thrall. His accomplishment—bringing the orcs together and throwing off the yoke of the demonic curse that had brought them so low—was even more impressive.

But Thrall was a unique individual among orcs. At their heart, orcs were uncivilized beasts, barely able to comprehend speech. Their customs and mores were barbaric, their behavior unacceptable. Yes, Thrall had kept them in line, using what he learned while being raised among humans to bring a semblance of civilization to them, but Thrall was mortal. When he died, so would the orcs' temporary flirtation with humanity, and they would descend right back into the vicious animals that they were when Sargeras first brought them here.

However, Lady Proudmoore would not hear those words. Certainly, Kristoff had tried, but even the greatest of leaders had their blind spots, and this was hers. She insisted on her belief that orcs could live in harmony with humans, to the point that she betrayed her own father.

That was when Kristoff realized that extraordinary action would need to be taken. The lady let her own father be killed rather than betray the trust of creatures who, beyond Thrall, would never return the favor.

Under other circumstances, Kristoff would never have done what he did. Every day, he awakened wondering if he had done the right thing. But every day, he also awakened in fear. From the moment he first came to Kalimdor through the end of the war and the founding of Theramore, Kristoff lived in abject terror that everything they had built would be destroyed. Aside from one fort on the Merchant Coast, the human presence on Kalimdor consisted of a small island off the eastern coast, surrounded on three sides by creatures who were at best indifferent, and at worst hostile to humans, and on the fourth by the Great Sea.

Despite his fears, despite his advice, the lady constantly took actions that favored the orcs to the detriment of humans. She claimed it was to benefit the alliance, that they were stronger united than they would be apart. The truly tragic thing was that she believed it.

But Kristoff knew better. And when Lady Proudmoore proved herself incapable of seeing the bigger picture, the very bigger picture that Kristoff had trained all his life to see, he got outside help.

Duree poked her shriveled head into the chambers. "Sir, the scrying stone from Northwatch is getting all glowy. I think it's got a message."

Dryly, Kristoff said, "That's usually what that means, yes." He got up from behind the lady's desk and went out into the throne room, where the stone was kept. Presumably, that was either Lorena or Davin informing him that the former had finally arrived, her troops having gotten there that morning. Kristoff's plan to have Lorena already in place when the troop carrier arrived was dashed by the airship's having mechanical problems that delayed its takeoff, plus the troop carrier benefited from a strong wind that hastened its arrival.

Walking up to the stone, which sat on a pedestal in the southwest corner of the throne room, Kristoff saw that it was indeed alight with the crimson glow that indicated that its counterpart at Northwatch had been activated and used.

Hesitating for a moment, Kristoff grabbed it. As expected, it sent a painful shock up his arm that almost forced him to drop it. The glow dissipated concurrently with the shock, followed by Major Davin's voice. It sounded like Davin was deep inside a cave and shouting toward the mouth.

"Lord Chamberlain, it's my sad duty to inform you that Colonel Lorena's airship has yet to report. Spotters saw the airship, but it was heading northeast. The troops have arrived, but I don't know what the colonel had in mind for 'em. Please advise."

Kristoff sighed as he put the stone back on its pedestal. "Damn that woman!"

"What woman?" Duree asked.

"Colonel Lorena. Who did she take with her on the airship?"

Without hesitating, the old woman called up the answer from memory. Peculiar though her manner might have been, the woman was incredibly efficient. "Major Bek, Captain Harcort, Captain Mirra, and Lieutenant Noroj. Oh, and Corporal Booraven."

Frowning, Kristoff asked, "Why did she bring a corporal along?" He had specifically told the colonel to have her senior staff on the airship and to send the troops along by boat. Then a memory started niggling at him. "I know that name from somewhere."

Duree, bless her, came to his rescue. "She's the one they called the good-luck charm, back during the war. A sensitive, if I'm rememberin' right—can sniff out magic at a hundred paces."

"Right, of course." Kristoff remembered that Booraven—who had been a private during the war—not only was able to detect demons that couldn't be seen with the naked eye, but also could tell when someone had been possessed by a member of the Burning Legion. She also was always able to find Lady Proudmoore, or any other wizard, a skill several generals made use of when the lady was difficult to track down during a chaotic campaign.

At once, Kristoff realized what Lorena had in mind. "Damn her!" Letting out a long sigh, he muttered, "And damn myself as well."

"What was that, sir?" Duree asked.

"Nothing," Kristoff said quickly. He couldn't afford to explain things to Duree. "That'll be all."

Sounding confused, Duree said, "All—all right, sir." Looking at him strangely, she left.

For his part, Kristoff stared out the large window. It was hazy today, and he couldn't see more than a league or two out on the Great Sea.

Belatedly, Kristoff realized that the mistake was truly his own. He had let the colonel's hostility toward him—which had always been there, going back to the days of the war—affect his own reactions to her. He treated her with the same contempt she treated him with, an indulgence that was acceptable, if sometimes counterproductive, when they both advised the lady, but suicidal when he sat on her throne. Part of the point of the symbolism of the raised throne was that the leader had to be above everything else—including the petty rivalries of the court.

The very arrogance that had done in Garithos and so many more before him, had done in Kristoff. If the chamberlain had treated Lorena with respect, she might have done as he asked. Because he didn't, she took Booraven with her to once again serve the purpose of finding Lady Proudmoore. That explained why she headed northeast: to Durotar, where the lady was taking care of the thunder lizards.

Much as it galled him, he had only one recourse. The plan had to go ahead, with some small variations. They might cause problems later, but by then the die would be cast. The only way for Jaina Proudmoore to see that the orcs were not to be trusted was to accelerate the inevitable war between them.

To that end, he picked up the stone once again, this time with both hands rather than one, which the stone registered as a desire to send a message. This time, the stone glowed blue. "This is Chamberlain Kristoff. I'm afraid our worst fears have been realized. Both Lady Proudmoore and Colonel Lorena have been taken by the foul orc cult known as the Burning Blade. The orcs must be made to pay for this. Major Davin, you are to take charge of all forces at Northwatch and prepare for war."

When he put the stone back down, the glow faded, its message sent through the aether to its counterpart in the keep.

After that, he retreated to the chambers to finish the work he had been in the middle of. However, the stink of sulfur permeated the air as soon as he arrived at the entryway, which meant that Zmodlor had arrived.

Galtak Ered'nash. **Report, Chamberlain.**

Kristoff wrinkled his nose, both because of the smell and in general disgust. He hated being involved with demons, and if the stakes weren't so high, he would just as soon run this creature through. But another lesson of leadership Kristoff had learned was that sometimes one had to make strange allies in order to serve the greater good of one's people. That was why Lady Proudmoore had taken the extraordinary step of bringing human and orc together in the first place, and why Kristoff now had to take the same step with Zmodlor. It was a temporary alliance with a minor demon who meant little in the grand scheme of things. In truth, Kristoff was using Zmodlor—playing on the creature's vanity and bowing and scraping before him in order for him to do precisely what Kristoff wished.

"All goes according to plan. The people of Theramore are primed to attack the orcs and destroy them."

Good. I will derive great pleasure from seeing those foul traitors wiped from this world.

"As will I." Kristoff meant those words. Zmodlor had been a useful ally to Kristoff because the two of them shared a fervent desire to rid the world of orcs. And when this was all over, and the orcs were no longer a factor, Kristoff fully intended to rid the world of Zmodlor as well. . . .

May our hearts' desires come to us sooner rather than later, Chamberlain. Farewell. *Galtak Ered'nash.*

Nodding, Kristoff repeated those two words in Zmodlor's native tongue that translated as: "All hail the Burning Blade."

SIXTEEN

Aegwynn watched with bitter amusement as Jaina Proudmoore tried to break the demonic wards. The girl had left Aegwynn's hut to go to the periphery of the wards—which were in the same location as the previous ones—and try to penetrate them from close up, at which Aegwynn didn't expect her to be any more successful.

Zmodlor obviously had no interest in meeting Aegwynn again, since he'd gone to the trouble to trap her here once Proudmoore dispersed the old wards. After all, as long as those wards, which were up due to Aegwynn's desire, were in place, Zmodlor had nothing to worry about. But if the wards went down, he'd be concerned, and so would have a backup in place.

Not that it mattererd. Aegwynn was long past the point of being able to fight demons magically.

After her latest failed attempt, Proudmoore reached into her cloak and pulled out some jerky. Almost unconsciously, Aegwynn nodded her approval. Whoever mentored the girl was sensible enough to teach her the practicalities. That was something Scavell, for all his brilliance, had never covered. It wasn't until the third time she collapsed from hunger following the pursuit of a demon that she thought to bring food with her on such missions.

Then the girl turned to face Aegwynn. "Perhaps if we combine our forces, we can do it."

"Not bloodly likely." Aegwynn laughed bitterly. "Adding my 'forces' to yours would give you the same result. My magical abilities have long since . . . atrophied." The word was inaccurate, but was sufficient for the purposes of answering Proudmoore's question. "A pity there's no one on the other side to serve as a conduit."

"A conduit for what?"

Aegwynn revised her estimate of Proudmoore's teacher back downward. "Don't you know Meitre's penetration spell?"

Proudmoore shook her head. "Most of Meitre's scrolls were destroyed ten years ago. I learned the ones that were salvaged, but that one doesn't sound familiar."

"Pity," was all Aegwynn would say. It mattered little to her whose wards were up, as long as they kept her safe here. She wanted nothing more than to live out the rest of her days away from the world she'd already done too much damage to.

"Why are you so weakened?"

Aegwynn sighed. She should have expected that.

Then again, perhaps Proudmoore needed to hear the *entire* story. Or at least, Aegwynn's own verison of it.

Twenty-five years ago . . .

Medivh had taken up residence in the tower of Kharazan in the Redridge Mountains, located in a series of hillocks. Surrounded only by vines and weeds—the old trees of the Elwynn Forest no longer made it up this far; they had died after Medivh took up residence—the tor on which Medivh had his keep was shaped exactly like a human skull.

Aegwynn found the shape to be sadly appropriate. She approached the place now on foot, having no desire to do anything to alert her son to her approach.

The Guardians of Tirisfal were dead. Orcs now rampaged throughout Azeroth. War had broken out all over the world. The source of all this?

Her own flesh and blood.

She didn't know how it was possible. She had sired Medivh to carry on her work, not unravel it.

Only when she arrived at the gates did she feel it. Her son was present, she knew that much, as were Moroes, the house servant, and the cook—though the latter two were both asleep in their respective chambers. But she felt another, one whose essence was intertwined with that of her son. One whom she had defeated centuries ago.

No longer bothering with her attempt to arrive subtly, she cast a wind spell that slammed into the gate, gale forces shattering the wood into a thousand pieces.

Her son stood on the other side. He had inherited Aegwynn's great height and her eyes; from Nielas Aran came his broad shoulders and elegant nose. His gray-flecked hair was tied back in a respectable ponytail, and he kept his salt-and-pepper beard well trimmed. His maroon cloak flowed behind him in the breeze.

Yet the being that stood before her was unrecognizable as her son. For, though her eyes saw Medivh, her entire wizardly being saw only Sargeras.

"How is this possible? I *killed* you."

Medivh laughed a demonic laugh. "Mother, are you truly that much of a fool? Did you really think that a mere girl could destroy the greatness that is Sargeras? He *used* you. Used you to make me. He hid within you, then—when you so ably seduced my father—transferred his essence to my fetus. He has been my constant companion—my mentor, the parent you never let me have."

Aegwynn couldn't believe it. How could she have been so blind? "You killed the council."

"Did you not always say that they were fools?"

"That's not the point! They didn't deserve to die!"

"Of course they did. You didn't teach me very much, Mother. You were always far too busy with your duties as Guardian to actually *raise* the son you brought into the world to succeed you. But one lesson you did impart on one of the rare occasions when you bothered to acknowledge my existence was that the council were fools. It was Sargeras who taught me what the final fate of all fools must be. You see, Mother, I learned *all* my lessons well."

"Stop pretending, Sargeras," she said. "Stop speaking in my son's voice."

Medivh threw his head back and laughed. "Don't you understand, little girl? I *am* your son!" He raised his hands. "And I am your end."

What happened next happened far more quickly than Aegwynn would have imagined. She remembered very little of the details, which was probably a mercy. All she knew for sure was that she had a harder and harder time countering Medivh's—or, rather, Sargeras's—spells and that he had an easier and easier time countering hers.

Weakened, battered, bleeding, Aegwynn collapsed to the stone floor of Medivh's keep, barely able to lift her head. Her son stood over her, laughing. "Why do you look so sad, Mother? I am exactly as you made me. After all, you sired me in order to circumvent the council and carry on your heritage. You did that. From the moment you destroyed Sargeras's physical form, thus freeing him to reside within you, your heritage was to facilitate Sargeras's will. Now you have fulfilled your purpose." He grinned. "One final poke in the eye to the council, eh?"

Aegwynn's blood turned to ice. Those were her thoughts upon Medivh's conception. She had never used that phrase aloud, certainly never to Medivh. She had indeed been a minor presence in his life at first, mostly for his own protection—she couldn't afford to let it be known that her son was in Stormwind, for fear that her enemies would use him against her. Indeed, she only revealed that she was his mother when he had passed puberty.

At that moment, she ceased all resistance. She no longer wished to live in a world that she had betrayed so thoroughly. In her eagerness to do her job right, to prove the council wrong in their dismissal of her, she had led to the victory of demonkind.

Not since she finished her apprenticeship had Aegwynn cried. The birth of her child, the death of her parents, the losses against demons—none of it had made her weep. She had always been stronger than that. Now, though, tears flowed freely down her cheeks as she looked up at her son, who laughed at her anguish.

"Kill me."

"And let you off the hook? Don't be a fool, Mother. I said I was your end, not your death. Allowing you to expire would not begin to atone for what you have done to me." Then he muttered an incantation.

Eight centuries ago, the council had given her the power of the Guardian, and it had been the most wonderful experience of her life. It was what it might have been like for a blind person to see for the first time. When she passed that power on to Medivh, it had been less wonderful, but still she had a feeling of satisfaction in creating her legacy, and the departure of the power had been smooth and pleasant, like drifting slowly to sleep.

Now, though, her power was being ripped from her by Medivh, and it felt like being struck blind, deaf, and dumb. Her entire body felt deadened—it was less like falling asleep and more like falling into a coma.

But she remained awake and aware of all that was happening. And she realized that if she stayed here, Medivh—or, rather, Sargeras—would keep her here. She would reside in the keep's dungeon, no doubt, able to see and hear all that went on, be made aware of every foul deed that her son performed in Sargeras's name.

She also realized something else—she was still young. Which meant that Medivh had not taken the de-aging magic from her.

That was her salvation, she realized. She gathered up the remaining tatters of her concentration and un-leashed the magic of the de-aging spells, grabbing it, harnessing it, and re-forming it into a teleport spell that would take her away from here.

Moments later, her hair having gone white, her skin having wrinkled, her bones having grown weaker, she found herself on Kalimdor, in a grassy region in the mountains of the continent's eastern coast.

Proudmoore's voice was quiet when she said, "That must have been terrible for you."

"It was." Aegwynn shuddered. In fact, it was worse

than that, but she had simply hit the high points for Proudmoore's benefit. She had actually tried to reason with Medivh, and tried to get an explanation from him as to why he did what he did—as if Sargeras needed a reason. But she saw no need to burden Proudmoore with that much—the point of the story was to show the depths of her own stupidity. She continued: "When I came here, I was able to use what little magic I had left to determine that there was no one around. I built my hut, planted my garden, dug my well. The wards didn't go up until Thrall and his people settled nearby."

"I'm not surprised." There was an odd tone to Proudmoore's voice when she said that—as if she knew something Aegwynn didn't.

"What's that supposed to mean?"

Before Proudmoore could answer, Aegwynn heard something. Proudmoore heard it too, as they both turned to face south. It sounded familiar, but it was a noise Aegwynn hadn't heard in years.

Moments later, her suspicion was confirmed: the noise was made by the displacement of air by a massive dirigible, which was now coming around one of the Bladescar peaks. It stopped right in front of the wards and hovered. Aegwynn assumed a mage—or at the very least, a sensitive—was on board.

A rope ladder fell from the undercarriage, and a figure in plate armor started to climb down. As the figure came closer, Aegwynn recognized the insignia on the armor as that of a colonel.

To her shock, the figure was a human female. She turned and gave Proudmoore a questioning glance.

The girl smiled. "If a woman can be a Guardian of Tirisfal, why can't a woman be a colonel?"

Aegwynn had no choice but to concede the point.

"Milady," the woman said as she came down off the bottom rung of the rope, "I'm afraid I bring bad news." She then looked askance at Aegwynn.

"Colonel Lorena, this is Magna Aegwynn. You may speak as freely to her as you would to me."

The colonel nodded and started to speak. Apparently the word of Jaina Proudmoore was enough for this colonel. Aegwynn grudgingly admitted to being impressed. A woman didn't rise to such a position without a great deal of hard work—she suspected that Lorena was twice as good as any male colonel, simply because she would have to be to succeed. If someone that talented trusted Proudmoore so implicitly, then Proudmoore may have been a more impressive specimen than Aegwynn had been willing to credit.

Perhaps there was something to the girl's hero worship after all.

Lorena said, "Ma'am, it is my firm belief that Chamberlain Kristoff is a member of the Burning Blade—that he has conspired to increase our forces at Northwatch and provoke the orcs into a conflict."

Proudmoore's face fell. "Kristoff? I don't believe that."

But the colonel spent the next several minutes explaining what had happened in Proudmoore's absence from Theramore.

When she was done, Aegwynn asked, "When did this Burning Blade start?"

"We're not sure," Proudmoore said. "We think it's related to a former orc clan. Why?"

"Because Zmodlor started a cult called the Burning Blade. In fact, the sword he was going to use to sacrifice the children he'd imprisoned was covered in oil and was to be set alight when the sacrifice commenced. Since Zmodlor is around, it's possible he was involved with those orcs as well."

Lorena spoke up before Proudmoore could respond to that. "Milady, why are you behind these wards? I brought Booraven with us to track you down, and she said there were wards up so we couldn't pass. But—why haven't you come out from behind them?"

"I'm afraid I can't. When I arrived here, I was able to penetrate the wards that had been put up, but they've been replaced with demonic wards from the very same Zmodlor that Magna Aegwynn was just discussing. I'm afraid I do not have the knowledge to bypass them."

"A pity," Aegwynn said. "If these were still my wards, I would let you through in an instant."

Snorting, Proudmoore said, "Don't be ridiculous— they were never your wards. They were Medivh's."

Aegwynn stared at Proudmoore in open-mouthed shock. "How did you—"

"When I first arrived here, I recognized the magic used for the wards as belonging to one of the *Tirisfalen*. But after I penetrated them, I realized I knew which of the *Tirisfalen* it was, because I'd encountered it before. As I tried to tell you earlier, I knew Medivh—it was he that brought human and orc to this land, and he that convinced us to ally against the Burning Legion. I know his magic quite well."

Lorena spoke before Aegwynn could respond. "Milady, with respect, time grows short. We must get you out of there. There *has* to be a way."

Proudmoore looked at Aegwynn. "There is. Teach me that spell of Meitre's." Pointing at the colonel, she added, "We now have the conduit."

"Very well," Aegwynn said, "if it means you'll leave me in peace."

"I'm afraid that's not possible."

Aegwynn blinked. "I beg your pardon?"

"You're coming with us."

Snorting, Aegwynn said, "Am I?"

"Yes. You are the magna, the Guardian who is all that stands between us and the demonic hordes. It is your responsibility to come with us."

"On what are you basing this ridiculous notion?"

"You said that Zmodlor built these wards. That means he is active—for all we know, he is responsible for the Burning Blade that is even now cutting through the alliance Thrall and I built at your son's behest. But you thought you defeated him eight centuries ago—

obviously you didn't finish the job, and it is your responsibility—"

"What do you know of responsibility?" Aegwynn cried. "For eight—"

"Yes, I know what you did, Magna, you've told me quite a bit about your failures, your deceits, your lies, your arrogance—but what you've also reminded me of is that you never once shirked your responsibility as Guardian. Everything you did—from facing Zmodlor to defying the council to siring Medivh—was done because you believed in what you did. Regardless of your mistakes, of your defeats, you never once shirked that responsibility. Until now." Proudmoore shook her head. "You asked me what I know of responsibility, and right now I'd say more than you, because you never had to be responsible to anyone save yourself. I have led people into battle, and I have ruled them when the battle was over—and right now, the people who have trusted me *need* me, and it may well be because of a demon *you* were supposed to have killed. I will not see everything we have built here be brought down by your self-pity, Magna."

"I believe I've earned the right to determine my own destiny."

"Because you brought Medivh back?"

Again Proudmoore had managed to stun Aegwynn with her perspicacity. She found herself unable to speak.

"We always wondered how Medivh came back from the dead after Khadgar and Lothar defeated him. It would have taken powerful magic to do so. I might have been able to do it, and so could one or two others, but if they had, they would have admitted it. You said you were drained by your fight with Medivh, but there is one thing that could substitute for that necessary power, and that's the bond between mother and son."

Aegwynn nodded, staring off into space at an indeterminate point on one of the Bladescar peaks. "With what was left of the de-aging magic, I was able to scry in the well water and learn what was happening. I saw my son killed by his apprentice and his best friend—and I saw Sargeras banished from him. So I spent years building up the power to bring him back. When I did, it almost killed me. That was why the wards were Medivh's—I no longer had the strength to cast them. Or anything else. I still don't." She turned to face Proudmoore. "That was my swan song, Lady Proudmoore. It cannot even begin to make up for all I have done wrong."

"I disagree. What you've done is sire a son who saved the world. It may have taken a while, but what he did was exactly what *you* would have done—what you conceived him to do. He went against the conventional wisdom and was proactive in fighting the Burning Legion by convincing Thrall and me to unite our forces. He didn't learn that from Sargeras, and he didn't learn that from whatever afterlife you retrieved him from—he learned that from *you*."

Lorena had been standing semipatiently during this

entire conversation, her obvious respect for Lady Proud-moore overcoming her soldier's desire for action. "Mi-lady—"

"Yes, of course," Aegwynn said, "your colonel is right. Zmodlor needs to be defeated—permanently this time." She sighed. "Prepare yourself, Colonel Lorena—this may hurt a bit. Lady Proudmoore, repeat after me."

And then Aegwynn taught Jaina Proudmoore Meitre's penetration spell.

SEVENTEEN

Thrall had spent the day hearing petitions. Most were for mundane matters that he would have thought his fellow orcs could handle on their own. Some were for disputes in which the two sides simply were not capable of agreeing, and so a neutral third party was required to settle them. In truth, it could have been anyone who settled them, but as Warchief, it was his duty.

When the last of the petitioners had left the throne room, Thrall rose from the animal-skin seat and paced the room, grateful for the opportunity to stretch his legs. He still had not heard from Jaina regarding the thunder lizards, but he had not received any more reports of rampaging thunder lizards, either, so he presumed that the situation was in hand. He just hoped she solved it soon so he could consult her about this Flaming Sword.

Kalthar and Burx both entered then. The latter spoke

in an urgent tone. "Warchief, there's someone here who has to talk to you. Now."

Thrall did not like the idea of Burx giving him orders, but before he could say anything, Kalthar gave Thrall a significant look.

"Do you think I should see this person, shaman?" Thrall asked.

"I do," Kalthar said quietly.

"Very well." Thrall stood his ground, having grown tired of the throne.

Burx went out and led one of the scouts in. A jungle troll, he was dressed in decorative armor and the mask that was traditional among those of the Darkspear tribe: feathers, wood, and paint combining with a triangular helmet to present a fearsome affect. By contrast, when he removed his helm, it was to reveal a friendly, open face, far gentler than one would expect from the fearsome Darkspears. Jungle trolls wielded powerful magicks, ones that no other race had ever been able to master—though Thrall knew of some humans who had tried and failed, at the cost of their souls—and the Darkspears had sworn allegiance to Thrall.

"This," Burx said, "is Rokhan."

The introduction was unnecessary—the troll's reputation preceded him as one of the finest scouts in Kalimdor.

Holding his helm under his arm, Rokhan stepped forward. "I'm afraid I be bringin' some bad news, mon. The humans, they be sendin' more troops to the Northwatch."

Thrall couldn't believe what he was hearing. "They're reinforcing?"

"That's what it look like, mon. I be seein' lotsa boats full'a soldiers, all headin' straight for the Northwatch. And they be sendin' one'a they airships up north, too, but it be goin' toward Bladescar."

Thrall frowned. "How many troops?"

Rokhan shrugged. "Hard to say, but they was at least twenty boats, and them things be carryin' at least twenty humans each."

"Four hundred troops," Burx said. "And this happened right after your friend Jaina went off to solve the thunder lizard problem that the *humans* caused. We can't wait for her to finish that, Warchief. I'm sure Jaina's intentions are good, but her people's aren't. And we *can't* ignore this!"

"Burx is correct." Kalthar spoke in a voice that sounded weary, and Thrall was reminded just how old the shaman was. "The maintenance of Northwatch Keep was a deliberate show of strength on the humans' part. However, this reinforcement in light of other recent events can only be an act of aggression, and one to which we must respond in kind."

"That was Admiral Proudmoore's stronghold." Burx hardly needed to remind Thrall of that, though that didn't stop him. "And now the subjects of Admiral Proudmoore's daughter are trying to finish his work behind her back."

Burx's words did not impress Thrall overmuch—but Kalthar's did. And Rokhan was the finest of his scouts. His observations were to be trusted.

"Very well. Burx, have Nazgrel assemble a garrison and send them into the Barrens. Have them take up position outside of Northwatch. Then I want you to take a fleet of our boats and send them downriver as well. Summon the trolls and have them do the same." He sighed. He had hoped that the days of fighting humans were past, but it seemed that old hatreds died very hard. "If the humans wish a fight, they will find us more than ready."

When Burx had finished giving instructions to Nazgrel and to the harbormaster, he returned to his home. He had preparations to make before he journeyed down the Great Sea in order to put an end to the human scourge once and for all.

It was while he was sharpening his ax that the smell of sulfur permeated his hut. He felt a warm sensation in the folds of his breeches, in the small inner pocket where he hid the talisman that Zmodlor had given him as a symbol of his allegiance.

Galtak Ered'nash. **Does all go according to plan?**

Burx hated the idea of swearing his allegiance to anyone save his own Warchief, but he played along and replied, "*Galtak Ered'nash.* It does. Thrall is sending troops by land and by sea. Within two days, our people will be at war with the humans. Within a week of that, the humans will be destroyed."

Excellent. You have done well, Burx.

"I just want to do what's right for the orcs. That's all I care about."

Of course. Both our causes are served by this war. *Galtak Ered'nash.*

As far as Burx was concerned, it was the lesser of two evils, was all. The demons were bastards, yeah, but they always had the orcs' best interests in mind. They brought the orcs to this world so they could rule it. It wasn't the demons' fault that the humans were able to do so well, to imprison them and make them forget who they were. Sure, the demons were using the orcs, but at least they never humiliated them.

Burx had grown up a slave. Humans regularly beat him, taunted him, defecated on him, and then forced him to clean up their messes while they laughed at him. They called him all manner of names, the kindest of which was "you greenskinned oaf," and they made sure to give him the most degrading tasks. Burx was never sure why he was singled out among the orcs on the estate for the horrible duties—no one ever bothered to tell him. Perhaps he was simply picked at random.

Compared to what he went through as a human slave, what the demons did was nothing. And if it meant cooperating with one of them to make sure that the plague that was humanity was wiped out, that was okay with Burx.

He owed Thrall everything and more, but Thrall could not get past his blind spot regarding the humans.

But then, Thrall had been well regarded by his master. True, Aedelas Blackmoore had had nasty plans for Thrall, but he had treated him a lot better than Burx's master did—better than most orcs, in fact.

Slowly but surely, Thrall was seeing the error of his ways. This troop amassment at Northwatch had finally done it. At this point, it was just a matter of time. Orc and troll warriors so close to human soldiers—it would be a powder keg.

Burx finished sharpening his ax, looking forward to seeing it run red with human blood.

EIGHTEEN

Lorena's chest pounded, and she had trouble breathing. Her plate mail felt as if it were constricting her.

But Lady Proudmoore and her friend—named Aegwynn, apparently, and whoever she was, the lady looked on her with more respect and awe than Lorena had ever seen her display before—were able to step through the demonic wards that kept them trapped. Apparently, they had to use Lorena's body on the other side of the wards to disrupt them. The colonel didn't understand any of it. Talk of magic usually just gave her a headache; all she cared about was whether or not it worked. When the lady cast the spell, it almost always did.

Lady Proudmoore then turned to the older woman. "Magna, I have a request."

"Oh?"

"Would you object to sharing your space witn some

thunder lizards? I can cast wards that will keep your house, your garden, and your well safe. And the highlands will keep them contained." She quickly explained the situation with the thunder lizards.

At that, the old woman laughed. "I have no objection whatsoever. I had a thunder lizard as a pet once."

Lorena's jaw fell open. "Please tell me you're joking."

"Not at all. It was shortly after my four hundredth birthday. After so long, the loneliness got rather overwhelming, so I decided to have a pet. I viewed domesticating a kodo as a challenge. I named him Scavell, after my mentor."

"Kodo?" Lorena asked with a frown.

Aegwynn shrugged. "It's what we called them then. In any event, I've always had a fondness for those beasts, and I'm more than happy to share my home with them."

"Thank you, Magna." Lady Proudmoore then turned to Lorena. "Give me a few minutes to complete the task that took me to Durotar in the first place, and then we will return to Theramore—I'll teleport the three of us. Instruct your soldiers to return to Theramore immediately via the airship." She smiled wryly. "I'm afraid teleporting the entirety of the airship after bringing the thunder lizards here will tax me beyond my capacity to be useful."

"Very good, milady," Lorena said with a nod.

"Thank you, Colonel." The lady said the words with a heartfelt smile, and Lorena felt a rush of pride. The

colonel had taken a huge risk coming here, trusting
Booraven's abilities to find Lady Proudmoore in orc
country, and hoping that the lady would not be angered
at her presumptuousness. But it seemed she had been
right to trust her instincts—and on top of that, she had
been instrumental in freeing the lady and her friend
from their prison.

While Lady Proudmoore closed her eyes and con-
centrated on her spellcasting, Lorena looked at the old
woman. "You're really four hundred years old?"

"Over eight hundred."

Lorena nodded. "Ah." She blinked twice. "You've aged
rather well."

Aegwynn smirked. "You should've seen me thirty
years ago."

Deciding that this conversation was getting far too
bizarre to suit her, Lorena instead went to the rope ladder to give Major Bek and the others their new instructions. Bek acknowledged the order, wished her the best
of luck, and prepared the dirigible for its return trip.

When she came back down the ladder, Lady Proudmoore had finished. As soon as Lorena had stepped off
the bottom rung, Bek ordered the ladder pulled back
up, and the airship began its journey back southward.

"The chamberlain's been spending most of his time
in the throne room." Lorena found herself unable to
keep the disdain out of her voice, then wondered why
she even tried. "And most of that's been on your
throne."

Lady Proudmoore nodded. "Kristoff always empha-sized the importance of sitting on the throne."

"A little too much, if you ask me," Lorena nodded. "In any event, I am ready."

Lorena braced herself. She'd been teleported only once, back during the war, and it had made her sick to her stomach.

Sure enough, the world turned upside down and in-side out, and Lorena felt as if her head had been re-moved and placed between her knees, while her feet were sticking up out of her neck.

A second later, the world normalized, and Lorena heaved. Dimly, as she bent over on the stone floor, she registered that this was Lady Proudmoore's throne room, and Duree was going to scream at her for retch-ing all over the floor.

"Milady!" That was Kristoff's voice. "You're back—and with Colonel Lorena. We were afraid you'd been taken by the Burning Blade. You'll be happy to know that we've reinforced Northwatch—which is good, as orc and troll troops are headed there by land and by sea. And who is this?"

Lorena heaved once again, her stomach clenching so badly it made being the conduit for the lady's spell seem heavenly by comparison.

"My name is Aegwynn."

"Really?" Kristoff sounded surprised, as if he knew who Aegwynn was. Lorena herself still had no idea, be-yond the fact that she was a very old woman.

"Yes. And while I'm no longer truly a *Tirisfalen*, I still know the stink of demonkind when I smell it, and it's all over you."

Though there was nothing left in her stomach, Lorena heaved again, wondering what a teeris fallen was.

"What are you talking about?" Kristoff asked.

"Please, Kristoff," the lady said, "tell me that Aegwynn is mistaken. Please tell me that you have not consorted with Zmodlor and the Burning Blade."

"Milady, it isn't what you think."

Her stomach having finished torturing her, Lorena was finally able to stand upright. She saw a rather interesting tableau. Kristoff stood in front of the throne, looking frightened. Aegwynn looked mildly peeved, which wasn't qualitatively different from how she'd looked since Lorena met her.

But in Lady Proudmoore, she saw something new: a cold fury. A storm seemed to be gathering behind her eyes, and Lorena found herself very grateful that the lady was on *her* side.

"Not what I *think*? What is it, exactly, Kristoff, that I should think?"

"The orcs must be eliminated, milady. Zmodlor has the same goal, and he is a minor demon. I have already put in place the sequence of events that will banish him from the world altogether when we are done."

" 'Done'? Done with what? Tell me what it is you've set in motion, Kristoff."

"A chain of events that will drive the orcs from this

world forever. It is for the best, milady. They do not belong in this world, and—"

"You *idiot!*"

Kristoff reacted as if he'd been slapped. Lorena was no less surprised than the chamberlain. In all the time she'd served under her, the colonel had never heard Lady Proudmoore speak with such vehement anger.

"Zmodlor is a *demon*. Do you truly believe that you will be able to stop him?" She pointed at the old woman. "This is *Aegwynn*, the greatest of the Guardians."

Aegwynn snorted at that, but both the lady and Kristoff ignored her.

"She was unable to completely defeat Zmodlor at the height of her power. What makes you think you'll fare better? And even if you could, *no* goal is worth risking an alliance with a demon. Their *only* purpose is to create havoc and desolation. Or was the destruction of Lordaeron not enough for you? Must Kalimdor follow in its wake once this war you seem bent on starting at Northwatch breaks out?"

"Besides," Aegwynn said, "even if you had the means to destroy or banish Zmodlor, you couldn't do it. You're in his thrall."

"That's absurd!" Kristoff sounded even more nervous now. "Ours is simply an alliance of convenience, and once the orcs are gone—"

"The orcs are our *allies*, Kristoff!" Lightning seemed to crackle around her golden hair, and a small breeze seemed to materialize at her ankles, billowing the lady's white cloak. "That alliance was forged in blood. And the demons are the enemies of everything that lives. How could you betray us—betray *me*—like that?"

Kristoff was sweating profusely now. "I swear to you, milady, it is not a betrayal. I was simply doing what was best for Theramore! The Burning Blade is simply a cult of warlocks under Zmodlor's direction that are bringing out the natural hostility toward orcs. They're doing nothing but abetting what's already there!"

"What about the orcs who are members?" Lorena asked.

"What?" Kristoff sounded confused.

"The orcs who attacked me and my troops at Northwatch, they were part of the Burning Blade—and they were orcs. How do they fit in?"

"I—" Kristoff seemed to be at a loss.

Lady Proudmoore angrily shook her head. "How many, Kristoff? How many will die to provide your perfect orc-free world?"

Now Kristoff seemed to be on surer ground. "Far fewer than if we wait until Thrall dies and the orcs revert to type. This was the only—"

"Enough!" Now the breeze kicked into high gear, and lightning shot out from the lady's fingertips.

Kristoff screamed a second later, clutching his left shoulder. Smoke started to wisp out from it between his fingers.

Instinctively, Lorena ran to Kristoff and ripped away the cloth of his shirt.

There was a tattoo on his shoulder blade of a sword on fire, identical to the ones Lorena, Strov, Clai, Jalod, and the others saw on the orcs they fought at Northwatch. The tattoo was now burning.

A second later, the tattoo was gone, leaving only charred flesh in its wake. Kristoff collapsed to the floor like a sack of suet, his eyes fluttering.

In a quiet voice, Aegwynn said, "Zmodlor's gone."

"Yes." Lady Proudmoore sounded calmer now. "And my casting that exorcism spell likely alerted him to the fact that we're on to him."

" 'M sorry . . ."

Lorena knelt down at Kristoff's side. His words were barely a whisper.

"Thought . . . what I did . . . of own free will . . . but Zmodlor . . . controlled . . . *everything*. So . . . sorry . . . sorry . . ."

The light faded from his eyes.

All three women stood in silence for several seconds.

The sad thing to Lorena was that Kristoff hadn't been a bad person, truly. He had done what he thought best for Theramore. He had been doing his duty. Of course, he had done it spectacularly badly, but his heart had been in the right place. That, in turn, made her feel guilty. There had been times when she wished Kristoff dead, but now that he *was* dead, she felt sad.

She looked at Lady Proudmoore. "We have to get to Northwatch. If we're lucky, the war won't have started yet, and maybe we can get the troops to stand down.

You've got to do it in person, though, milady—Major Davin won't take orders from anyone else."

Lady Proudmoore nodded. "You're right. I'll—"

"No."

That was Aegwynn. The lady gazed at her coolly. "I beg your pardon?"

"There's magic afoot here, Lady Proudmoore, and you're the only person in Kalimdor who can stop it. Your erstwhile chamberlain was right about one thing— Zmodlor is a minor demon. He was a sycophant of Sargeras's. He doesn't have the power to influence so many people—or to raze a forest and teleport the trees, if it comes to that. Those warlocks Kristoff mentioned are the source of all this—they're acting in Zmodlor's name, probably in exchange for rare scrolls or some other such thing." She shook her head. "Warlocks go after spells like an addict to a poppy plant. It's revolting."

"We don't have time to go on a hunt for a group of warlocks," Lorena said.

"Those warlocks are the source of all this, Colonel," Aegwynn said.

Lorena looked at Lady Proudmoore. "For all we know, milady, the fighting has already started. If it hasn't, it may at any second, if Kristoff was right about those orc and troll troops heading down. Once the fighting starts, it won't matter who or what caused it— there *will* be bloodshed, and once that line is crossed, the alliance will be permanently sundered."

Aegwynn also regarded the lady. "Time is of the

essence. You said yourself that Zmodlor knows that you're on to him. We have to strike *now*, before he has a chance to form a strategy against you. And you can't be in two places at once."

Then the lady smiled. It was a radiant smile, one that Lorena took as something of a relief after the anger she had displayed toward Kristoff. "I don't *need* to be in two places at once." She walked to the entryway of her chambers. Lorena and Aegwynn exchanged confused glances, and then followed.

When they walked in, they saw Lady Proudmoore rummaging through the scrolls on her desk, before finally saying, "Aha!"

She turned around and held up a rock that was carved into an intricate shape. Then it started to glow. . . .

NINETEEN

"Sir, the orcs, they've set up camp."

Major Davin started ripping out tufts of his beard, dress code be damned. "How many?"

Shrugging, Corporal Rych said, "Impossible to be sayin' for sure, sir."

Davin closed his eyes and counted to five. "Take a guess."

Another shrug. "Lookout, he be sayin' there's at least six hundred, sir—but hard to say for sure, sir. They be stayin' far enough back that they ain't violatin' no borders or nothin', but—"

At Rych's hesitation, Davin sighed and prompted him. "But what?"

"Well, sir, right now they just be *sittin'* there, but I don't think that'll be lastin', sir. 'Specially once those boats arrive."

Again, Davin sighed. It seemed that sighing was all he did these days. Dozens of boats carrying orcs and trolls alike were seen heading south on the Great Sea a day ago, heading right for Northwatch. They'd arrive within a couple of hours.

At that point, Davin would have a decision to make.

His instructions from Chamberlain Kristoff—who, with Lady Proudmoore compromised by these Burning Blade people, was in charge—were to hold Northwatch "no matter what."

Davin had no idea how he was supposed to do that.

He hadn't even wanted to be a soldier. True, he had an aptitude for violence that made him very attractive to the recruiter who came to his village as a boy, but he was also a tremendous physical coward. He managed to fake it through training, mostly by virtue of never actually being in danger. If it was just playacting, Davin had no difficulties at all. Use his sword on a straw dummy? No problem. But real combat against a flesh-and-blood foe? Then he was hopeless.

So the first time he had faced off against a person, he had thought he'd be doomed. But he had lucked out by being part of a particularly talented platoon. Davin had done little when he had faced off against the renegade dwarves who had come to his village to try to escape dwarven justice after a failed attempt to overthrow the existing government. But the rest of his platoon had done quite well, capturing or killing all the dwarves. Davin had been able to bask in the reflected glory of his comrades.

Then the Burning Legion had come.

It had been awful. People had died all around him. Lordaeron had been destroyed. Humans and orcs had fought side by side. The entire world had turned upside down. Davin had never understood why Lady Proudmoore had chosen to ally with the orcs—they were devils, not significantly better than the demons themselves—but nobody had asked Davin his advice.

The worst day had been in some forest somewhere. Davin hadn't even known *where* it was, only that he was there with the tattered remains of his platoon, and they were trying to find a demon stronghold so some wizard or other could learn its secrets. Davin's job was simple: protect the wizard. Everyone else was seeking out the stronghold.

Unfortunately, they found it. The demons didn't take kindly to the notion.

As soon as they came, their eyes aflame, Davin panicked and hid behind one of the oaks. He left the wizard exposed, and while the mage tried his best to defend himself, eventually one of the demons set him afire. While Davin watched from the safety of his arboreal hiding place, the wizard he was supposed to be protecting screamed in agony and died very very slowly.

Somehow—Davin was never entirely clear why—the demons overlooked him. Perhaps they didn't deem Davin to be a threat, which was certainly true. Either way, though, when his platoon was wiped out and the demons buggered off to wherever it was demons buggered off to, Davin ran back to base camp, expecting to be excoriated for being such a coward, but willing to face the consequences, as long as he wouldn't have to go out and face such a thing again.

Instead, they hailed him as a hero for surviving the deadly onslaught and coming back to report what had happened.

Then they promoted him.

Davin was stunned. He was no hero; he was, in fact, the exact opposite. But every attempt to clear the air just resulted in his being considered unduly modest. It was maddening—instead of being relieved of combat, he was put in charge of other troops.

Shortly thereafter, the war was kind enough to end, thus sparing Davin the embarrassment of having to actually lead troops into a battle he was incapable of fighting. The Burning Legion was driven back to whatever hell they had come from, and Davin was given *another* promotion, this time to major. After Admiral Proudmoore's arrival and subsequent death, Davin was put in charge of Northwatch Keep.

Until recently, he had welcomed the duty. Northwatch was fairly peaceful, and while Davin's cowardice made combat an impossibility, he did fine at administration.

Assuming, of course, that nothing went wrong.

Davin didn't especially like Colonel Lorena, but he really wished she were here right now, instead of off with the Burning Blade. For one thing, she was a lot better at running a garrison of troops than he was. Unlike

Davin's, Lorena's promotions had actually been based on merit.

For another, if the Burning Blade could get *her*, not to mention Lady Proudmoore, what hope did *Davin* have?

Oreil came running in, his too-big armor clanking with each step. "Major Davin! Major Davin! The orcs're moving! It happened as soon as the boats docked!"

Davin sighed yet again. "When did the boats dock?"

"Didn't anyone tell you?" Oreil blinked a few times. "Oh, wait, I was supposed to do that. I'm sorry, sir, but I got all overexcited. Please don't court-martial me."

Getting up from his desk and heading out the door, Davin said, "Private, right now a court-martial is the least of your worries."

Slowly, Davin walked down the narrow staircase that led to the ground floor of the tower at Northwatch's center. Northwatch was built on an uneven hill that sloped down to the Great Sea. The eastern border of the keep was a stone wall that had been built between two of the hillocks; the buildings that made up North-watch were on the western side of the wall, with a beach lined with palm trees on the eastern side.

As he approached the archway that led through that stone wall and onto the beach, Davin saw orcs and trolls.

Many many orcs and trolls.

Their boats were all tethered to poles that had been sunk into the sand. There were dozens of them, each with a full complement of about a dozen trolls or orcs.

Some wore animal skins; others wore the heads of vicious beasts as helms. All of them were armed with axes and broadswords and morningstars and maces, and other weapons that all appeared at first glance to be bigger than Davin himself.

"So this is it," he muttered. "We're going to die."

"What was that, Major?" one of the troops guarding the archway asked.

Shaking his head quickly, Davin said, "Nothing." Somehow, the major managed to force himself to keep putting one foot in front of the other. As he passed through the archway, his boots started to sink into the sand with each step.

Dimly, he registered that dozens of troops had fallen into line behind him. He took a quick glance back to see that several of them were forming a skirmish line in front of the wall, and others were taking up position atop it. Davin was grateful that *someone* had the wherewithal to give that order, and he briefly wondered who it was.

Turning back to face the new arrivals, he said, "I'm Maj—"

He cut himself off. His voice was breaking.

Clearing his throat, he started again. "I'm Major Davin. I'm in charge of Northwatch Keep. What business do you have here?"

For a brief moment, Davin entertained the hope that the orcs would say they were just passing through for a brief respite and would be gone within the hour. He hoped it as fervently as he had hoped that his return from the massacre of his platoon would result in his being cashiered out, and this hope looked to have as much likelihood of becoming reality as the previous one.

Sure enough, the biggest, scariest looking one stepped forward. (Davin was willing to concede that this one seemed biggest and scariest *because* he was the one who stepped forward.)

"I am Burx. I speak for Thrall, Warchief of the Horde and Lord of the Clans. This keep of yours violates our alliance with you people. You've got one hour to take it down and get rid of any and all traces of your presence here."

Davin sputtered. "You—you can't be serious. There's no way we can take down the entire keep in an hour!"

Burx smiled. It was the type of smile that a large predator might have right before it pounced on its small, defenseless prey. "If you don't comply with this order, we'll attack. And you'll die."

Of that last part, Davin had very little doubt.

TWENTY

Jaina had sent Aegwynn and Lorena to the small dining hall that was reserved for high-ranking officers and officials of state. For practical purposes, according to Duree, the little old woman who assisted Jaina, the latter mostly had meant the now-deceased Kristoff and Jaina herself. The young mage had given Aegwynn permission to enter there, as well. When Duree objected, Jaina pointed out that a Guardian was of greater rank than a head of state.

For her part, Jaina had retreated to her chambers—she too needed to eat, but she had to do it while working, trying to determine the location of the warlocks. Lorena wanted to join her troops at Northwatch, in case Thrall was unable to stem the tide of battle, but Jaina refused. For one thing, she trusted Thrall. For another, she needed Lorena as physical protection when they confronted Zmodlor and his minions, especially since Kristoff had sent Jaina's official protection, the Elite Guard, to Northwatch.

But Jaina needed to work in solitude, so she sent the old Guardian and the young colonel to the dining hall.

When the steward came by, Aegwynn asked for only a salad and some fruit juice; Lorena ordered a meat platter and boar's grog. Aegwynn had never heard of the latter, and Lorena explained that it was an orc drink.

Letting out a long breath, Aegwynn said, "How times have changed."

"What do you mean?"

"It wasn't that long ago that orcs were nothing but the minions of the demons I had dedicated my life to stopping. They were monsters, berserkers that ravaged the countryside in the name of Gul'dan, who was in turn acting for Sargeras. The notion of humans drinking an orc beverage is . . . radical, to say the least."

Lorena smiled. "Yes, but isn't 'that long ago' a relative term when discussing someone as old as you?"

Aegwynn chuckled. "A fair point."

"You're *really* a thousand years old?"

Smiling wryly, Aegwynn said, "Give or take a century."

Lorena shook her head. "Magic. I've never understood it—always hated it, to be honest, even when it's being used in my service."

Aegwynn shrugged. "I've never wanted any other life for myself *but* as a wizard. From when I was a little girl, it was how I always answered those tiresome questions about what I wanted to be when I grew up. The adults always looked at me strangely when I said that—wizards were always *men*, after all." That last was said with a certain bitterness.

"So were soldiers. I grew up with nine brothers, and they were all soldiers just like my father. I didn't see any good reason why I shouldn't be one, either." Lorena chuckled. "I got the same strange looks, believe me."

The drinks arrived a moment later, as did Aegwynn's salad. Lorena held up her mug. "Would you like a taste?"

Boar's grog smelled about as wretched as the animal for which it was named. Her nose wrinkling, Aegwynn politely declined. "I'm afraid I haven't had a drink of alcohol in—well, centuries. Mages can't afford the loss of mental acuity, so I lost the taste for it some time ago." She held up her mug, which was apparently a mixture of the squeezings of three or four different fruits. "This is as strong a concoction as I'm willing to imbibe."

"Makes sense." Lorena threw back a big gulp of her grog. "Me, I can drink four of these things before I even notice. Always had a high tolerance." She grinned. "When I was a rookie with the Kul Tiras City Guard, I always used to drink the men in my barracks under the table. We started having contests with the other barracks, and I was always the secret weapon." She laughed. "I quadrupled my income on bets alone during that year."

Aegwynn smiled as she nibbled on her salad. She found herself enjoying talking with this woman—an emotion she wouldn't have credited herself capable of feeling only a day ago. She had been thoroughly convinced that she had no more use for the company of other people.

The steward brought a pile of assorted meats, cooked to a fine brown. Aegwynn only recognized some of them, but she assumed the livestock on Kalimdor was different enough to account for that. It had been years since she ate meat, and, unlike the smell of the colonel's drink, the smell of the meat was almost intoxicating. As a mage, it was her constant companion—the exhaustive requirements of casting spells required regular infusions of protein—but since her self-imposed exile to Kalimdor she hadn't the wherewithal to hunt her own meat, nor the physical need to consume it, so she had become a vegetarian.

"Mind if I have a bite?" To Aegwynn's surprise, she asked the question shyly—another emotion she didn't think herself still capable of.

Pushing the plate to the center of the table they sat at, Lorena said, "Be my guest."

As Aegwynn hungrily chewed a piece of what looked like boar sausage, Lorena asked, "I have to ask, Magna—what's it like?"

"It's Aegwynn," she said while chewing her sausage. "I stopped being the Guardian when I passed on the power to my son. And I'm certainly unable to fulfill the responsibilities of the title now." She swallowed. "What's *what* like?"

"Living for so long. I'm a soldier, born and bred, and I've known from the beginning that I probably won't live to see my fortieth year. You've reached your fortieth decade—twice over. I just can't imagine that."

Aegwynn let out a long breath—which now smelled of boar sausage, an odor that was still more pleasant than the grog named after the same animal. "There really wasn't much time to reflect on things. Guardian is a full-time job, sadly. Demonic threats have been a constant since before *I* was born. The attacks became more overt in recent times, which probably made things easier. But when I wasn't stopping demons I was covering up evidence of their perfidy. Most people didn't know about it—or about me—and the council preferred to keep it that way." She shook her head. "It's odd—I defied them in so many ways, but that particular credo I kept to. I wonder if that was a mistake. Yes, people probably *felt* safer not knowing the truth, and more people died in the recent wars—but the demons have also been more roundly defeated. Your Lady Proudmoore and her orc friend did more damage to the entirety of demonkind than has been done in thousands of years."

"We're contentious beings, mortals." Lorena smirked. "Give us a foe to fight, and we'll go after it with our dying breath. And beyond, if needs be."

"Indeed. Colonel—may I have another piece?"

Lorena laughed and said, "Help yourself."

Taking another piece of meat—this time one she didn't recognize—Aegwynn wondered what would happen after this was over. She found the prospect of returning to her little hut in the Bladescar Highlands to be less enthralling than she would have thought. Jaina had been correct—humans and orcs had built a life here, and it was because of Medivh. Which meant, ultimately, it was because of her. Perhaps it would be best if she reaped the fruits of her labors. . . .

Before she could ponder further, Jaina entered the dining hall. "I've found them. We must move quickly."

The young mage looked ragged. Aegwynn stood up. "Are you well?"

"A little tired. I'll be fine," Jaina said dismissively.

Aegwynn pointed at the plate of meat. "Eat something—you'll be of no use to anyone if you collapse, and I know better than anyone what happens to spells that aren't cast with full concentration."

Jaina opened her mouth, then closed it. "You're right, of course, Magna."

Lorena leaned over to Jaina. "She doesn't like to be called that."

At that, Aegwynn barked a laugh. She was really starting to like this colonel.

After Jaina wolfed down some of Lorena's meat—Aegwynn was amused to realize that Lorena had gotten the smallest share of her own meal—the lady said, "The

Burning Blade is operating out of a cavern atop Dread-mist Peak."

Lorena winced. "Oh, great."

Looking at Lorena, Aegwynn asked, "What's the problem?"

"Dreadmist Peak is aptly named. The upper regions of the mountain are choked with this orange mist."

Dismissively, Jaina said, "It's residuum from an ancient demonic curse on the place. That's probably why Zmodlor chose it—that, and its location, since it's about equidistant from both Orgrimmar and Theramore. In any case, my magicks will protect all three of us from the effects of the mist."

"Good," Lorena said emphatically.

"Also, Duree was able to find this." Jaina pulled a familiar-looking de-sealed scroll from inside her cloak and handed it to Aegwynn.

She took it, noted that the broken seal was that of the *Tirisfalen*, then opened it and laughed. The scroll's lettering was in her own handwriting.

Handing it back to Jaina, Aegwynn said, "That's my refinement of the banish-demon spell. I wrote that three hundred years ago, after Erthalif died and I got access to his redoubt." She shuddered at the memory of the old elf's library, which would have had to be several orders of magnitude neater before it could be considered merely a mess. It took her and Erthalif's staff ten weeks just to organize the scrolls, scrub away the desiccated food and drink, and chase off the vermin. When she found the notes taken by the legendary elf wizard Kithros on the moving of objects from one realm to another, Aegwynn had been able to incorporate them into a more efficient spell for banishing demons. "I daresay if I'd had this eight hundred years ago, we wouldn't be dealing with Zmodlor today."

Jaina put the scroll back in her cloak. "Actually, no. I checked up, and it turns out that you were completely successful in banishing Zmodlor the first time. But when the Burning Legion attacked, they recruited many demons, including ones that had been banished by the *Tirisfalen*. When the war ended, several stragglers managed to stay in this world even when the legion was driven back."

"And Zmodlor was one of them?" Aegwynn asked.

"Yes." Jaina nodded.

Unsheathing her sword—and sounding to Aegwynn remarkably gung-ho for someone who was so appalled by the notion of going to this Dreadmist place—Lorena said, "Milady, if I may ask—what are we waiting for?"

"This warning," Jaina replied. "I was unable to scry too closely, for fear of being detected, so I'm not sure what kind of protection Zmodlor and his warlocks will have. We must be ready for anything." She turned to face Aegwynn. "Magna—Aegwynn—you need not accompany us. It may be dangerous."

Aegwynn snorted. This was a hell of a time for her to say that, and a bit of a reversal from her earlier lecture on her responsibilities as Guardian. Then again, at the time they had thought that she had failed in her banishment of Zmodlor, and now they knew that was not the case. Yet, she still felt some measure of responsibility. "I was facing dangers far worse than that little twerp of a demon when your great-great-grandparents were infants. We're wasting time."

Jaina smiled. "Then let's go."

TWENTY-ONE

Corporal Rych had no idea who it was who started the fighting.

One moment, he was standing there in the skirmish line in front of Northwatch Keep's wall, Private Hoban on his left, Private Allyn on his right. They stood about twenty paces behind Major Davin. The major himself was amazing, just standing up to that orc like the war hero he was, not scared or nothing. Did them all proud, the major did.

The next moment, the skirmish line was shattered, and orcs, trolls, and humans were getting into it. All around him, he heard the clang of metal on metal, and the shouts of both sides imploring their fellows to kill their foes.

Not that Rych minded all that much. The orcs had their nerve, they did. Wasn't enough they had to pull their stunts in trade at Ratchet, leading to a good man like Captain Joq getting pinched by the bruisers, now they had to come and try to kick them out of their rightful place in Northwatch.

Rych wasn't putting up with *that*, he wasn't.

He unsheathed the family claymore. Father was part of the Kul Tiras Irregulars back in the day, and used the claymore to good effect. After he died of the flu, Mother joined up and killed plenty. She died fighting the Burning Legion, and the claymore came to Rych— which was a relief, as the longsword he'd been using was crap.

Although he wasn't as good with it as Mother, he was better than Father was, and he intended to spill plenty of orc and troll blood with it.

One of the trolls came right at him, holding up a huge cleaver. Rych parried the cleaver, then kicked the troll in the stomach. That trick always worked on the drunks he used to clear out of Mowbry's Tavern back home.

Unfortunately, trolls had tougher bellies, and this one just laughed and swung again with the cleaver.

Blood pooled in the sand under him, but Rych couldn't spare a glance to see whose it was as he parried the cleaver again.

"You've had this comin' a long time," the troll said as he lifted the cleaver.

While the troll was wasting time saying this, Rych stabbed the troll in the chest.

His foe falling to the sand as Rych removed the claymore, he turned to see that the blood was from both

Hoban and Allyn, who lay dead in the sand, blood pouring from multiple wounds. An orc was charging toward the keep gates, blood dripping from his ax. Screaming, Rych ran for the orc and stabbed the greenskin in the back.

" 'Ey! Human!"

Rych whirled around to see another orc.

"You killed Gorx!"

"Gorx killed my friends," Rych said with a snarl.

"Yeah, fought 'em, but you stabbed 'im inna back!"

Not seeing the big deal, Rych said again, "He killed my *friends*!"

Raising his greatsword, the orc said, "Well, now I'm gonna kill *you*!"

The greatsword was a *lot* bigger than Rych's claymore, but that meant it took the orc a lot longer to swing it, as he had to wind up to strike, which gave Rych plenty of time to either dodge or parry. An attempt at the latter resulted in an impact of blade on blade that sent convulsions through his entire body, leaving Rych to embrace the efficacy of the former.

Or so he thought—the fourth time he dodged the greatsword, he bumped into Private Nash. That caused Nash to turn around in surprise, leaving him open to an attack from an orc's pulverizer.

Anger got Rych's blood boiling. It wasn't enough that these orcs had to attack, now they were making him screw up his fellow soldiers. Screaming incoherently, he ran at the orc with his claymore.

The orc stepped aside to his left, holding out his greatsword, which cut through Rych's chest plate and stomach as he ran past. White-hot agony sliced through his torso, and his scream became even more incoherent. He flailed his claymore about with his right hand while clutching his injured chest with his left.

Suddenly, the claymore stopped short and wouldn't move. Wincing in searing pain even as he did so, Rych turned to his right to see that the claymore had impaled the orc's head.

"Serves you right," he managed to blurt out through clenched teeth.

He yanked the claymore out of the orc's skull, which shot a lot more pain through his chest. For some reason, the sounds of battle had dimmed, and all Rych could hear was a persistent roaring in his ears.

Using the family weapon as a makeshift walking stick, he stumbled forward in the sand, looking for more orcs to kill.

TWENTY-TWO

A moment ago, Aegwynn had been standing in Theramore.

A moment ago, Lorena had taken a very deep breath and looked apprehensive. Aegwynn remembered the colonel's words about how she hated magic—not to mention her nausea in response to teleporting last time. Briefly, Aegwynn wondered if it was such a good idea for Lorena to have eaten prior to this.

A moment ago, Jaina Proudmoore had looked determined.

Now, they stood at the mouth of a cave surrounded by a foul-smelling orange mist, leading Aegwynn to understand why Lorena had been so unenthusiastic about coming here. The orange miasma hung in the air like the worst kind of fog. Aegwynn almost felt weighed down by it.

Aegwynn had long since grown inured to the effects of teleportation, so the only disorientation she felt was related to the mist. She shot a glance at Lorena, who looked a bit pale, but was still holding her sword before her, ready for anything.

Jaina, however, looked as pale as Lorena, which was not a good sign.

However, Aegwynn said nothing. There was no going back now, and the last thing Jaina needed was someone acting like a mother hen. Aegwynn herself had certainly hated it when someone—usually Scavell, or, when they were sleeping together, Jonas, or one of the council—fussed over her when she was exhausted and still had to do battle, so she saw no reason to inflict that on Jaina now.

Still, there was cause for concern. Jaina had cast four teleport spells today that Aegwynn knew about—herself to Bladescar, the thunder lizards to Bladescar, the three of them back to Theramore, and the three of them to this cave—plus scrying Zmodlor's location, doing whatever she did to keep the thunder lizards under control, and inuring the three of them to whatever this mist did under normal circumstances. That much casting in one day alone would start to take its toll, and for all Aegwynn knew there was more besides.

As Jaina led the way through the mouth of the cave, Aegwynn wondered when she had stopped thinking of the golden-haired mage as "Lady Proudmoore"—or "that annoying little girl"—and had started thinking of her as "Jaina."

Aloud, she said, "Zmodlor's here, all right." She shuddered. "He's everywhere." The demon had obviously set up shop in this cave, and his essence was in the very rock. She hadn't been so overwhelmed by foulness since she confronted her son at Kharazan—though some of the feeling might have been due to the mist. It only added to the general unpleasantness of the dank cave. Jaina cast a light spell that allowed them to see, but all that served to do was make the mist brighter. Then again, Aegwynn had no interest in getting a better look at the damp walls, stalactites—the points of which threatened the top of her head—and uneven stone floor.

After they'd walked twenty paces into the cave, Aegwynn stiffened. "There's—"

"I've got it," Jaina said. She muttered a quick incantation.

Aegwynn nodded. Both she and Jaina had sensed the simple entrapment spell. A low-level spell that any first-year apprentice could cast successfully, it was probably designed mostly to stop any stray animals or people from wandering in unannounced. It was unlikely that someone would be walking about up in this nightmare, but Aegwynn had seen stranger in her time. It would be just like some wolf or a lunatic mountain-climbing dwarf to come up here and meander into the cavern just as Zmodlor and his minions were in the middle of casting something that required concentration. Best not to take chances.

However, dismantling the spell might well serve as an alarm. Aegwynn made sure to keep Lorena and her sword and Jaina and her magicks between herself and the rest of the cave at all times.

Moments later, Lorena cried, "Get down!"

Not being a fool, Aegwynn immediately dropped to the cold floor. Lorena did likewise.

Jaina, however, stood her ground and held up her hands. The fireball that roared toward her looked about to consume her—

—but it stopped an arm's-length before doing so, dissipating instantly.

Clambering to her feet, Aegwynn said, "I'd say they know we're here."

"Indeed." Jaina's voice was only a whisper.

Oh yes.

Aegwynn sighed. The voice seemed to come from everywhere—a popular demon trick. "Can the theatrics, Zmodlor. We're not your brainless minions, and we're not impressed."

Aegwynn! What a pleasant surprise. I had thought you had long since died at the hands of your son. How fortunate that I get to do it myself, instead. I owe you for what you did to me.

Even as the demon ranted, Aegwynn heard strange cackling noises.

"I know that laugh." Lorena sounded disgusted. "Grellkin."

Sure enough, a score of little demons, covered in fur that matched the color of the mist, scampered toward them.

Moving forward to protect Aegwynn and Jaina both, Lorena said, "I really really hate these guys." Then she charged ahead and attacked.

The fuzzy creatures were too much for one woman to handle; luckily, there were two women to do so. Jaina cast several spells that had various effects on the grellkin. Some had their fur catch fire. Others stopped breathing. Others were blown into the cave walls by sudden gale-force winds in the enclosed space. None of these were particularly impressive spells, but they were all minor enough that they allowed Jaina to conserve her power.

But that was only the first wave. After the first twenty were killed, twenty more replaced them.

"This is a distraction," Aegwynn said.

"Yes," Jaina said. She cast another spell that disintegrated the twenty grellkin.

Another line of ten were behind them.

"Colonel," Jaina said quickly, "can you handle these?"

Lorena grinned. "Watch me."

"Good."

As the colonel waded into the demonic attackers, Jaina closed her eyes and almost stumbled. Aegwynn moved to grab her. "Are you all right?"

With refreshing honesty, Jaina said, "No. I can cast the banishment, but only if I don't cast anything else. Lorena has to take care—"

A piercing scream echoed throughout the cavern as Lorena managed to stab the last three grellkin with one thrust of her sword. She yanked the sword out, and the creatures collapsed to the floor. Staring at the ichor-encrusted blade, Lorena sighed. "I'm never going to get these stains off."

I suspect that will be the least of your problems.

This time the voice didn't come from everywhere: it came from right in front of them.

The orange mist parted, which Aegwynn knew couldn't possibly be a good sign. It revealed the massive form of Zmodlor.

TWENTY-THREE

Panic rooted Davin to the very spot. Around him, his soldiers were dying, their limbs being hacked off, blades slicing through their chests, axes cutting off their heads.

And Davin simply stood there, waiting to die.

He had thought for sure that as soon as the fighting commenced, Burx would cleave him in two with his ax. But the orc got sidetracked by a couple of other soldiers who leapt in to defend their commanding officer. Davin wasn't entirely clear what he had done to inspire such loyalty.

After that, no one came after him. Orcs and trolls picked humans to fight, or vice versa, and somehow Davin, standing closer to the shoreline than anyone else, got ignored.

The body of a troll fell at his feet. The body of Corporal Barnes flew past in a high arc and landed in the water. Davin wondered why Barnes's orc opponent felt the need to throw Barnes so far, then decided that he really didn't want to know.

Then the world exploded.

An earthquake shook the ground so heavily that it accomplished what panic had prevented: it got Davin to move, albeit to fall to the ground.

Though there hadn't been a cloud in the sky a moment ago—in fact, it had been a clear, sunny day—now the skies had gone dark, and thunder and lightning struck the ground with an ear-splitting crack.

Davin heard a rumble and looked to the shoreline to see a massive wave start to rise up. In all the time Davin had been assigned to Northwatch, he'd never seen a wave that big hit the shore that wasn't due to the wake of a boat.

However, this wave was as high as the keep's wall—and it was about to come crashing down right on Davin.

Quickly, he tried to clamber to his feet, but his boots could not gain purchase on the sand, and he fell on his face. Spitting sand out of his mouth and trying not to inhale all the sand in his nose, Davin gave in to the inevitable and braced himself by shoving his fists down into the sand.

The water slammed into him, almost uprooting him from the spot, but his armor and anchored hands kept him weighted down. He wondered how the other soldiers who were less secure fared; he didn't much care about the orcs and trolls. Mostly, though, he wondered if he'd ever be able to breathe again.

Seconds later, the water flowed back in the other direction. The wave had washed the sand off his face, though he was now drenched, water matting his hair and causing his beard to weigh heavily on his face.

"You have shamed me this day, my warriors!"

Davin rolled over onto his back and looked up. The skies were still dark, save for one spot, in which hovered a dirigible.

Briefly, Davin allowed himself to feel hope—perhaps the airship belonged to Colonel Lorena, who had freed herself and Lady Proudmoore from the Burning Blade. This sudden meteorological nightmare could easily have been the lady's doing, after all. They had come to rally the troops, drive the orcs back, and save the day.

Then he took a closer look at the dirigible, and his heart sank. The canvas was decorated with several bizarre symbols, all of which the major recognized as being orcish. At least two of those symbols were mirrors for ones he saw on armor and weaponry that orcs carried during the war—not to mention on the troops that were currently killing his soldiers. Davin's platoon commander during the war had said that they were the orc equivalent of coats-of-arms for their various clans.

Davin had never been a particularly religious sort. The only time in his life he'd ever prayed was when he was hiding behind the tree and praying that the demons wouldn't notice him. That particular prayer was answered, but Davin didn't want to push his luck, so he never prayed again.

Now, though, he prayed that he would survive this day. Somehow, he found the strength to get to his feet.

The words Davin had heard had come from the airship. A rope ladder fell toward the ground and went taut as the orc who owned the voice that spoke the words climbed down.

When the orc arrived on the shore, the orcs all around—or at least the ones Davin could see in his peripheral vision, as his eyes were focused on the new arrival—raised their weapons in salute. The major also noticed that this orc had blue eyes, and at once he realized who it had to be. Until now, Davin had never actually met the orc Warchief, and he recalled that Thrall was also a shaman of great power. Like Lady Proudmoore, he could easily be responsible for this inundation.

Holding aloft his two-handed hammer with one hand—this, Davin knew, was the legendary Doomhammer that had once belonged to Orgrim, Thrall's mentor—the orc cried out, "I am Thrall, Warchief of Durotar, Lord of the Clans, Leader of the Horde! I come to you now to say that—" He pointed at Burx. "—this orc *does not speak for me!*"

Over the past half-dozen years, Davin had had plenty of congress with orcs. There was the war, of course, and Northwatch's location on the Merchant Coast meant that plenty of orcs came through the area.

In all that time, Davin had never seen quite the expression on an orc's face that he now saw on Burx's.

"Warriors of Durotar, you will stand down!" Again he pointed at Burx, but this time with the hammer. "This foul creature has consorted with a demon in order to bring about war between our people. I will not violate our alliance to suit the needs of the very creatures who tried to destroy us."

Burx snarled. "I have been your loyal servant!"

Thrall shook his head. "Several warriors who served with you have reported a talisman you carry in the shape of a sword afire—that is the symbol of the Burning Blade. According to Jaina—as well as an ancient wizard who has allied herself with the humans—all those who carry that symbol are in the thrall of a demon known as Zmodlor, who is attempting to foment discontent on Kalimdor and sunder our alliance. As ever, demons do nothing but use us and then destroy us."

Indicating Davin with his weapon, Burx said, "*These* are the bastards who tried to destroy us! They enslaved us and humiliated us and *denied us our heritage!*"

His voice a calm contrast to Burx's near hysteria, Thrall said, "Yes, some of them did—and they did so because of demons who drained our very souls and forced us to fight their war on the people of this world, a war that we eventually lost. But we have thrown off those shackles and risen to be as strong as ever. And the reason *why*, Burx, is because we are *warriors*. Because we are pure of spirit. Or, rather, most of us are. I cannot call pure one who consorts with foul creatures to cause orcs to violate their word."

The orcs and trolls all looked at Burx with a mixture of surprise and revulsion. There were a few, Davin noticed, who seemed confused. One of the latter spoke up. "Is this true, Burx? You made a deal with a *demon?*"

"To wipe out the humans, I'd make a deal with a *thousand* demons! They gotta be destroyed!"

Then, to accentuate his point, Burx charged right at Davin.

Every instinct in Davin's body cried to run away, but he could no more make his legs move now than he could when the wave hit. He saw Burx's ax as the orc swung it upward in preparation for cleaving Davin's skull.

But before he could complete the swing, Burx's entire body convulsed. He stopped moving forward and fell to the sand. As he did so, Davin saw that Thrall had struck Burx from behind with Doomhammer.

"You have brought disgrace to Durotar, Burx. You have caused the dishonorable deaths of orc and troll and human warrior alike. This blight can only be eliminated by your death. As Warchief, it is my solemn duty to carry out that sentence."

Thrall raised Doomhammer over his head and then brought it down hard on Burx's head.

Davin flinched as blood and gore splattered all over the sand, onto Thrall, and onto Davin himself. He was, however, too frightened to actually move to wipe any of it off, not even the blood that mixed in with the water on his left cheek or the bits of skull in his beard.

Thrall likewise made no attempt to remove the stains of Burx's death from his person—and he was much more fouled by it. Davin supposed that it served as a badge of honor to an orc. The Warchief stepped forward and said to Davin, "You have the apologies of Durotar for this traitor's behavior, Major, and for this terrible battle that has happened this day. I will not permit the Burning Blade to influence my people anymore. I hope the same will be said for you."

Not trusting his mouth to work properly, Davin simply nodded.

"We will depart. I am sorry we did not arrive soon enough to avoid bloodshed, but first I had to order the troops amassed on land to stand down. We all shall return to Durotar, and not attack you again." The Warchief stepped forward. "Unless you give us reason to."

Again, Davin nodded, more eagerly this time.

He continued to stand there as Thrall ordered his troops to gather their dead and wounded and return to their boats and set sail northward for Kolkar Crag. Davin remained standing with his boots sunk into the sand, bits of Burx's blood, skull, and brains on various portions of his armor and person, as Thrall climbed back up the ladder to his airship, and both airship and waterborne vessels proceeded northward.

Davin was stunned to realize that, for the second time, his prayer had been answered, and he was starting to think there might be something to the whole praying thing.

He was equally stunned at how quickly everything had changed—all because of Thrall's words. Yes, his rather spectacular actions got everyone to stop fighting for a minute, but that would've been only temporary. Thrall's words were what convinced the orcs and trolls to stop fighting and retreat.

Much as he hated to admit it about an orc, Davin was impressed.

Finally, a captain whose name Davin couldn't for the life of him remember, asked, "Orders, Major?"

"Ah—stand down, Captain." He let out a breath he hadn't even realized he was holding, suddenly feeling very exhausted. "Stand down."

TWENTY-FOUR

Not five minutes ago, Aegwynn had urged Zmodlor to cease his parlor tricks. The disembodied voice trick was probably menacing to the average person, but it was a simple trick that any first-year apprentice could pull off. So it didn't impress Aegwynn all that much.

Now, seeing the huge, leathery-skinned, bat-winged, flame-eyed Zmodlor standing before her, she realized she should have kept her mouth shut. Demons on the whole were not pretty creatures, but Zmodlor was hideous even by their standards.

Surrounding the demon were eight hooded figures. These, presumably, were the warlocks, who were chanting rhythmically.

Jaina reached into her cloak and grabbed the scroll. Aegwynn was grateful, as it meant this would be over soon. Now that Zmodlor had revealed himself, Jaina would be able to cast the banishment.

Suddenly, Jaina screamed and fell to the floor.

"Jaina!" Aegwynn ran to the young mage's side. Lorena, good soldier that she was, moved to stand between the demon and Jaina.

Sweat beaded on Jaina's forehead as she managed to get to her knees. Through clenched teeth, she said, "Warlocks . . . blocking the spell."

This close, Aegwynn could feel the warlocks' spellcasting. It was fairly weak, though there were about a dozen of them, which added power to their spells. Still, a mage of Jaina's stature should have been able to punch through that.

Unless, of course, she'd overextended herself.

Jaina was struggling—Aegwynn could feel it—but she was losing ground to Zmodlor's minions.

This is even better than I'd hoped. I'll make sure that the orcs are blamed for Proudmoore's death. It will send the humans into a frenzy. Nothing will stop them from going to war, and without her to guide them, they'll lose—but not before they kill as many orcs as possible. It will be glorious!

"Like hell," Aegwynn muttered. There was only one thing for her to do.

It had been almost four years since she brought Medivh back. That had drained all her magic at the time, as she'd told Jaina—but the magic never went away forever. Two decades after she had escaped to Bladescar, she had built up enough magical power to bring back her son. While she hadn't regained anywhere near that much in the four years since, she might well have enough to do what was necessary. If not—well, she'd lived almost a full millennium. As Lorena had so eloquently pointed out, that was a lot more than most people got.

Sweat was now pouring down Jaina's face. She was still kneeling, fists clenched and resting on her thighs. Aegwynn could feel the spell that she herself had written struggling to push past the blocks the warlocks were putting up.

Down on one knee at Jaina's side, Aegwynn grabbed the younger woman's left fist with both hands. She closed her eyes, gathered up her thoughts, her power, her very life essence. Focusing it, molding it, moving it, she channeled it all into her arms . . . then her forearms . . . then her hands . . .

And then to Jaina.

Fatigue rather suddenly overwhelmed her. Her bones felt heavy in her skin, her muscles ached as if she had just run a race, and her breaths came in shallow gasps. Ignoring all of it, Aegwynn continued to focus, willing her life, her magic, her very soul to Jaina Proudmoore.

Jaina opened her eyes. Normally an icy blue, they were now a fiery red.

No!

Simultaneously, both Aegwynn and Jaina said, "Yes!"

You cannot stop the Burning Blade! We will prevail over all, destroying everything in our path, and then we—aaaaaaaaaAAAAAAAARRRRRRRRGH!

Zmodlor's screams echoed—not only off the walls,

but from the mouths of the warlocks, who felt sympathetic agony through the bond the demon had with them. Though Aegwynn's vision was fading, she saw Zmodlor's hideous body twist and contort, ichor spewing from wounds that suddenly ripped open.

A wind kicked up as the air itself was rent asunder by the spell Aegwynn had written—a portal to the Twisting Nether—pulling Zmodlor's body into the tear.

Nooooooooo! I won't let you trap me aga—

The demon's words were cut off by his head being sucked in.

But the screams continued from the warlocks, even as the ground shook under Aegwynn's unsteady legs. Moments later, they stopped as they, too, were sucked into the Twisting Nether, where they would suffer anguish several orders of magnitude worse than what they had planned for the residents of Kalimdor.

The tear closed—but the cavern was still shaking.

Showing a soldier's capacity for stating the obvious, Lorena said, "We've got to get out of here!"

But Aegwynn couldn't make her limbs move. Her arms and legs felt like dead weights, and it took all her energy just to keep her eyes open.

One of the stalactites ripped from the cave roof with a sharp crack and impaled the floor less than a handsbreadth from where Aegwynn and Jaina both knelt.

Aegwynn heard Jaina start to mutter the incantation for the teleport spell.

Then she passed out.

EPILOGUE

O nce again, Lady Jaina Proudmoore stood atop the butte on Razor Hill, gazing out over Durotar.

Soon, she heard the low, steady rumble that heralded the arrival of Thrall's airship. This time, the Warchief came with an honor guard, most of whom remained in the undercarriage while he climbed down the rope ladder to greet Jaina. One warrior, whom Jaina did not recognize, came down after him. When they alighted on the butte, the warrior stood three paces behind Thrall, holding his ax at the ready in front of him.

Smiling wryly, Jaina said, "Do you not trust me, Thrall?"

Thrall returned the smile. "My own closest advisor betrayed me, Jaina. I think it's best if I remain alert at all times—and with someone watching my back."

"A wise move."

"Is the threat truly ended?"

Jaina nodded. "It would appear to be. Zmodlor and the warlocks who performed his magicks have been banished to the Twisting Nether. Even the Burning Legion would be hard-pressed to liberate them—and so minor a demon would hardly be worth the effort."

"Well done. I only wish it could have been accomplished before blood was spilled unnecessarily." Thrall's hand went to his belt, from which hung a talisman in the shape of a flaming sword. Jaina assumed it belonged to Burx, the advisor who had allied himself with Zmodlor, just as Kristoff had. According to Major Davin's report—provided along with his letter of resignation—Thrall had killed Burx in front of a large cadre of orc and troll warriors for consorting with the Burning Blade.

Sighing, Jaina said, "We were very lucky, Thrall. Zmodlor may have been responsible for this, but he simply brought up hatreds that were already there. Look at how easily your people and mine took to killing each other at Northwatch."

"Indeed. It was far easier for our people to cooperate with the Burning Legion as a common enemy. Now . . ." His voice trailed off.

Silence hung in the air for a few moments before Jaina spoke again. "Before, I said that after this crisis was solved, we would speak of a treaty between our people."

"Yes. If this alliance is to outlive the two of us—and it must, if both humans and orcs are to survive—then we must formalize our alliance."

"I suggest we meet one week from today at Ratchet—it's a neutral port, and we can work out the specifics."

"Agreed. I shall bring Kalthar—he is the wisest of us."

Jaina couldn't help herself. "Wiser even than the Warchief?"

Thrall laughed. "Far far wiser than he. It will be done, Jaina."

"Excellent. Farewell, Thrall. I will see you in a week."

"Farewell, Jaina. May we come out of this crisis stronger than ever."

Nodding, Jaina cast the spell that would bring her back to her chambers.

Aegwynn was there waiting for her. It had taken the old woman a few days to awaken after she passed out in the cave, and Jaina had feared for a time that the Guardian would not recover at all.

Jaina had barely enough left in her to teleport the three of them to a spot a ways down on Dreadmist Peak, away from the mist. She could not take them any farther than that; somehow, she had dredged up enough to contact Theramore and have an airship come to fetch them.

Although Jaina was fairly ragged when the dirigible rescued them, Aegwynn was as weak as a kitten. A hot meal and a nap, and Jaina was fine. Aegwynn, however, needed a lot longer than that. The Chief Healer's initial prognosis was not good, but after a few days, he declared her to have the constitution of an elf.

Sure enough, she recovered fully. She now sat in the guest chair in Jaina's chambers. "About time you got back."

"I see you've recovered fully, Magna—your tongue included."

Aegwynn laughed. "So it would seem."

Jaina fell more than sat in her own chair, feeling rather tired. She wouldn't have minded a few days to recover from the ordeal herself, but had been unable to take the time. There was no chamberlain to fob off some of the work on to. Duree had handled as much as she could, but as useful as she was, she could not deal with any of the more complex aspects of running Theramore. Lorena had been somewhat more helpful, at least in military matters, but she too had no skill with other aspects of government. So Jaina was unable to devote herself fully to resting up—much to the irritation of the healer—which left her fatigued.

She regarded Aegwynn, who stared back with her deep green eyes. It frightened Jaina that their entire victory over Zmodlor was due to the happenstance of her choosing the Bladescar Highlands as the place to relocate the thunder lizards. Even if she had discovered that Zmodlor was responsible, without the erstwhile Guardian, she never would have been able to defeat the demon and his minions.

"I want to thank you, Mag—Aegwynn. Without you, all would have been lost."

Aegwynn simply bowed her head in response.

"I suppose that you'll want to return to Bladescar?"

"Actually," Aegwynn said with a lone small smile, "no."

Jaina blinked. "No?"

"I'd like to return long enough to retrieve some things, and pick from the garden one last time before the thunder lizards trample all over it. But I've been out of the world for far too long. I think it's time I started living in it again. Assuming that the world will have me, at any rate."

"Most definitely." Jaina sat up in her chair. She had hoped that Aegwynn would feel that way, but had not in her wildest dreams believed that those hopes would become reality. "As it happens, I have an opening for a chamberlain. It's a position that requires knowledge, insight, and a willingness to put me in my place and tell me off when I need it. I'd say you qualify in all regards— especially the last part."

Laughing, Aegwynn said, "Certainly, though the first two are arguable. Still, I suppose I gained *some* knowledge and insight in a thousand years." She got to her feet. Jaina did likewise. Aegwynn held out her hand. "I accept."

Returning the handshake, Jaina said, "Excellent. Thank you again, Aegwynn. You won't regret this."

"No, but you might." Aegwynn broke the handshake and sat back down. "Here's my first piece of advice to you as your chamberlain: Kristoff was right. Zmodlor was a minor demon. He didn't have the brains to come up with something like this."

Jaina frowned. "I thought you said he started the Burning Blade."

"Yes, but just as a means to cull souls. A plan of this complexity is far beyond him. You yourself said that Zmodlor wasn't the only demon left behind after the Burning Legion was driven back."

Knowing the answer to the question, Jaina felt the need to hear it from the Guardian's lips nonetheless. "What is it you're saying, Aegwynn?"

"I'm saying, Jaina, that this is probably not the last we've heard from the Burning Blade."

ABOUT THE AUTHOR

Keith R.A. DeCandido is the author of over two dozen novels, plus whole bunches of novellas, short stories, eBooks, comic books, and nonfiction, in a wide variety of media universes. In addition to *Warcraft*, he's played in the worlds of *Star Trek* (in all its incarnations, plus some new ones), *StarCraft*, Spider-Man, the X-Men, *Buffy the Vampire Slayer, Serenity, Farscape, Andromeda, Resident Evil, Xena,* and a whole lot more. He is also the author of the high-fantasy police procedural *Dragon Precinct,* and the editor of many anthologies, most recently the award-nominated *Imaginings* and the *Star Trek* anthologies *Tales of the Dominion War* and *Tales from the Captain's Table.* His work has journeyed to several bestseller lists, and has received critical acclaim from *Entertainment Weekly, Publishers Weekly, TV Zone, Starburst, Dreamwatch, Library Journal,* and *Cinescape,* among others. He lives in New York City with his girlfriend and two lunatic cats. Find out too much about Keith at his official website at DeCandido.net, keep up with his ramblings on LiveJournal under the rather goofy user name of "kradical," or just send him silly e-mails at keith@decandido.net.

Available now from
Pocket Star Books

STARCRAFT®
GHOST
NOVA

A novel by

KEITH R.A. DeCANDIDO

THE PREQUEL STORY TO
BLIZZARD ENTERTAINMENT'S
HIGHLY ANTICIPATED
STARCRAFT: GHOST

TURN THE PAGE FOR A PREVIEW. . . .

As soon as she felt Cliff Nadaner's mind, Nova knew that she could destroy her family's murderer with but a thought.

She'd spent days working her way through the humid jungles of the smallest of the ten continents of Tyrador VIII. *Funny how I tried so hard to avoid this planet's twin, and now I wind up here,* she had thought when the drop-pod left her smack in the middle of the densest part of the jungle—before the rebels had a chance to lock onto the tiny pod, or so her superiors on the ship in high orbit insisted. The eighth planet in orbit of Tyrador was locked in a gravitational dance with the ninth planet, similar to that of a regular planet and a moon, but both worlds were of sufficient size to sustain life. They also both had absurd extremes of climate, thanks to their proximity to each other—if Nova were to travel only a few kilometers south, farther from Tyrador VIII's equator, the temperature would lower thirty degrees, the humidity would disappear, and she'd need to adjust her suit's temperature control in the other direction.

For now, though, the form-fitting white-with-navy-blue-trim suit—issued by her teachers at the Ghost Academy when her training was complete—was set to keep her cool, which it did, up to a point. The suit covered every inch of her flesh save her head. The circuitry weaved throughout the suit's fabric might interfere with Nova's telepathy, and since her telepathy was pretty much the entire reason *why* she was training to become a Ghost, it wouldn't do to interfere with *that*. This suit wasn't quite the complete model she would be using when she became a Ghost—for one thing, the circuitry that allowed the suit to go into stealth mode had yet to be installed. Once that happened, Nova would be able to move about virtually undetected—certainly invisible to plain sight and most passive scans.

But she wasn't ready for that yet. First she had to accomplish this mission.

The suit's design meant that sweat dripped into her eyes and plastered the bangs of her blond hair to her scalp. The ponytail she kept the rest of her hair in was like a heavy damp rope hanging off the back of her head. *At least the rest of my body is comfortable.*

The suit's stealth mode would probably have been redundant in this jungle in any case. The flora of Tyrador VIII was so thick, and the humid air so hazy, she only knew what was a meter in front of her from the sensor display on the suit's wrist unit.

Intelligence Section told her that Cliff Nadaner was headquartered somewhere in the jungle on this planet. They weren't completely sure where—though still only a trainee, albeit not for much longer, Nova had already learned that the first half of IS's designation was a misnomer—but they had intercepted several communiqués that their cryptographers insisted used the code tagged for Nadaner.

In the waning days of the Confederacy, Nadaner was

one of many agitators who spoke out against the Old Families and the Council and the Confederacy in general. He was far from the only one who did so. The most successful, of course, was the leader of the Sons of Korhal, Arcturus Mengsk—in fact, he was so successful that he actually did overthrow the Confederacy of Man and replaced it with the Terran Dominion, of which he was now the emperor and supreme leader. Nadaner did somewhat more poorly in the field of achieving political change, though he was very skilled at causing trouble and killing people.

Days of plowing through the jungle had revealed nothing. All Nova was picking up was random background radiation, plus signals from the various satellites in orbit of the planet, holographic signals from various wild animals that scientists had tagged for study in their natural habitat, and faint electromagnetic signatures from the outer reaches of this continent or one of the other nine more densely populated ones. All of it matched existing Tyrador VIII records and therefore could be discarded as not belonging to the rebels. And now she was reading a completely dead zone about half a kilometer ahead, at the extreme range of the sensors in her suit. *This is starting to get frustrating.*

She had completely lost track of time. Had it been four days? Five? Impossible to tell, since this planet's fast orbit gave it a shorter day than what she was accustomed to on Tarsonis, with its twenty-seven-hour day. She supposed she could have checked the computer built into her suit, but for some reason she thought that would be cheating.

Let's see, I've got enough rations for a month, which means ninety packs. I've been eating pretty steadily, more or less on track for three squares a day, and I've gone through fourteen packs, so that makes—

Then, suddenly, it hit her. *A dead zone.*

She adjusted the sensors from passive scan to active scan. Sure enough, they didn't pick up a thing—nothing from the satellites, nothing from the animal tags, nothing from the cities farther south.

Nothing at all.

Nova smiled. She cast her mind outward gently and surgically—not forcefully and sloppily, the way she always had back in the Gutter—and sought out the mind of the man who killed her family.

In truth, Nadaner had not personally killed her family. That was done by a man named Gustavo McBain, a former welder who was working a construction contract on Mar Sara when the Confederates ordered the destruction of Korhal IV—an action that killed McBain's entire family, including his pregnant wife Daniella, their daughter Natasha, and their unborn son. McBain had sworn that the Confederacy of Man would pay for that action. However, instead of joining Mengsk—himself the child of a victim of Korhal IV's bombardment with nuclear weapons—he looked up with Cliff Nadaner's merry band of agitators.

Nova learned all that when she killed McBain. Telepathy made it impossible for a killer not to know her victim intimately. McBain's last thoughts were of Daniella, Natasha, and his never-named son.

Now, three years later, having come to the end of her Ghost training, her "graduation" assignment, which came from Emperor Mengsk himself, was to be dropped in the middle of Tyrador VIII's jungle and to seek, locate, and destroy the rest of Nadaner's group. Mengsk had even less patience for rebel groups than the government his own rebel group had overthrown.

Within five minutes, she found the mind she was looking for. It wasn't hard, once she had a general location to focus on, especially since they were the first higher-order thoughts she'd come across since the drop-pod opened up and disintegrated. (Couldn't risk Dominion tech getting into the wrong hands, after all. If she completed her mission, they'd send a ship to extract her, since then they could land a ship without risk, as Nadaner's people would be dead. If she didn't complete it, she'd be dead, and her suit was designed to do to her what was done to the drop-pod if her life signs ceased. Couldn't risk Dominion telepaths getting into the wrong hands, either, dead or alive.)

It was Nadaner. Also about a dozen of Nadaner's associates, but their thoughts were focused on Nadaner—those that were focused at all. The man himself was chanting something. No, singing. He was singing a song, and half his people were drunk, no doubt secure in the knowledge that no one would find them in their jungle location, with its dampening field blocking any signals. It probably never occurred to them that an absence of signals would be just as big a signpost.

Complacent people are easier to kill, she thought, parroting back one of Sergeant Hartley's innumerable one-sentence life lessons.

She was to kill them from a distance, using her telepathy. Yes, her training was complete, and she should have been able to take down Nadaner and his people physically with little difficulty—especially since half of them were three sheets to the wind—but that wasn't the mission.

The mission was to get close enough to feel their minds clearly and then kill them psionically.

That was the mission.

For the next two hours, Nova ran through the jungle, getting closer to her goal. After her "graduation," the suit would be able to increase her speed, allowing her to run this same distance in a quarter of the time, but that circuitry hadn't been installed, either.

The hell with the mission. That bastard ordered McBain and the rest of his little gang of killers to murder my family. I want to see his face when I kill him right back.

Soon, she reached the dead zone. She could hear Nadaner's thoughts as clearly as if he'd been whispering in her ear. He'd finished singing and was now telling a story of one of his exploits in the Confederate Marines before he got fed up, quit, and started his revolution, a story that Nova knew was about ninety percent fabrication. He had been in the Marines, and he had been on Antiga Prime once, but that was where his story's intersection with reality ended.

With just one thought, she could kill him. End him right there. *That is the mission. You don't need to see his face, you can feel his mind! You'll know he's dead with far more surety than if you just saw him, his eyes rolling up in his head, blood leaking out of his eyes and ears and nose from the brain hemorrhaging. Kill him now.*

Suddenly, she realized what day it was. *Fourteen packs, which means the better part of three days.*

Which means today's my eighteenth birthday.

It's been three years to the day since Daddy told me I was coming to this very star system.

She shook her head, even as Nadaner finished this

story, and started another one, which had even less truth than the first. A tear ran slowly down Nova's cheek.

It was such a good party, too . . .

Constantino Terra had long since given up throwing surprise parties for his daughter. She always knew they were coming and ruined the surprise. *In retrospect,* he thought, *that should've been the first clue.* But other evidence had also presented itself, and soon Constantino realized that his darling Nova was a telepath.

Were he someone else, Constantino would have been forced to give in to the inevitable and turn his daughter over to the military for proper training. But the Terra family were not "someone else," they were one of the Old Families, descended from the commanders of the original colony ships that had brought humanity to this part of space from Earth generations ago. The Old Families did not turn their daughters over to anyone they didn't want to. And Constantino refused to put his little girl through that.

Her mother agreed. There was little that Constantino and Annabella Terra agreed upon, but that Nova should stay out of government hands was assuredly one of them. Not that they needed to agree on anything save that they remain married. Like most Old Family marriages, theirs was based on financial expediency, a union of two fortunes that would work better together than apart, and would also produce worthy heirs. Those heirs were created by an injection of Constantino's seed into Bella's body, thus saving him the distasteful task of sleeping with the wretched woman. He had his mistress for that, just as she had her jig, as was proper. Constantino had heard whispers among the servants that Bella was growing tired of her jig and seeking out other household employees for her sexual sport. But then, he'd also gotten word of similar rumors regarding him and his beloved Eleftheria, and he would never betray her trust. The mistress-husband bond, and the jig-wife bond, for that matter, was far too strong and important to the household for him to consider sundering it.

Instead of his daughter spending her fifteenth birthday in some government facility being trained to use her psionic talents as a tool against the alien threats the Confederacy now faced, she was instead being thrown the finest party since—well, since the last time one of the Old Families' children had a birthday. It was a competition, in many ways, with each family throwing a more and more outlandish shindig to prove that they loved their children the most.

As a result, the domed roof of the penthouse atop the Terra Skyscraper was decked out as it had never been decked out before. The dome had been polarized to provide an optimum view of the city of Tarsonis without interference from the sun. (The Terra family's building was one of the few buildings that had a virtually unobstructed view, matched only by that of Kusinis Tower and, of course, the Universal News Network Building.) A massive chandelier, six meters wide, hung in midair atop the dome, supported by state-of-the-art antigrav units guaranteed not to fail. (The guarantee was that Constantino would drive the manufacturer to complete ruin if it did fail.) Food from all across the Confederacy was laid out, as expected, but he actually managed to get his hands on Antigan buffalo meat and a limited supply of

Saran pepper slices. The price for the latter two items was higher than the aggregate salaries of any ten of Constantino's employees, but it was worth it for his little girl.

All the important people were there—at least three representatives from each Old Family on Tarsonis, and a few from offworld—and UNN had dutifully sent all its gossip reporters, and even one of its news reporters, a woman named Mara Greskin. Constantino smiled at her presence. *She must have cracked off somebody to get assigned to cover a birthday party.* Usually such occasions were fodder only for gossip columns; news reporters considered such assignments beneath them, which was why Greskin simply had to have annoyed somebody important—or gotten in UNN editor-in-chief Handy Anderson's doghouse.

Then again, if they're covering this, it means one less paranoid story about how aliens are going to wipe us out. It seemed all UNN was talking about these days were the horrors in the Sara system and the emergence of a strange alien threat. Constantino knew more than UNN did, of course—for example, that there were, in fact, *two* alien species fighting a war that the human race somehow got caught in the middle of—which only made him worry more, especially since Arcturus Mengsk and his band of butchers in the Sons of Korhal were using the invasion as a propaganda tool to stir uprisings on planets from here to Antiga Prime.

In the face of all this, Constantino threw a party. It was, after all, his daughter's birthday, and he was damned if he'd let Mengsk or alien scum distract him from *that*.

Nova was becoming a woman. According to the girl's nurse, she had started what the nurse insisted on calling "her monthly time"—as if Constantino wasn't familiar with the female anatomy and its functions—and she had started to develop a woman's chest. Soon, the prepubescent disdain for the opposite sex would give way to hormonal imperatives. *Which means an endless array of unsuitable suitors for my little girl.*

In truth, Constantino was looking forward to it. There was nothing quite so satisfying as watching a young man trying desperately to impress one of the most powerful men in the Confederacy and failing miserably, that failure compounded by Constantino holding him to an impossible standard. He'd already gone through it with Nova's older sister, Clara—now engaged to young Milo Kusinis—and was looking forward to it again with Nova.

Now, Nova stood in the center of the domed space, wearing a beautiful pink dress that had a ruffled neck, the white ruffles opening like a flower beneath her chin, a formfitting top, and a huge hoopskirt that extended outward half a meter in all directions and came to the floor. She walked with such grace and ease that the skirt's hiding of her feet made it seem as if she were floating when she walked. (Other girls achieved the same effect by attaching gliders to their shoes, unseen under the skirt's voluminous mass, but Nova, the darling girl, had always felt that to be cheating.) She wore very little makeup, simply enough to highlight her green eyes; her smooth skin needed no cosmetic enhancements, and so far the ravages of adolescence had not blemished her visage.

Her normally straight blond hair had been curled for the occasion and piled atop her head elegantly. Constantino made a mental note to apologize to Rebeka. He had doubted the hairdresser's word when she said Nova would look marvelous with curls; he should have known better after all these years. After all, Rebeka had made even Bella look presentable on more than one occasion.

All around them, the partygoers were partaking of the food on the tables, the servants ably refilling any plates that were in danger of emptying. The punch bowl remained three-quarters full no matter how much of it was imbibed—and, it seemed, old Garth Duke was determined to imbibe most of it himself; Constantino made a mental note to have Boris keep an eye on him in case he started undressing again—and the empty glasses and plates were whisked away. As ever, Constantino had the most efficient servants. If he ever had an inefficient one, he didn't have that one for long.

There were those who expressed confusion at his employing of human servants—most of whom were among the younger, newer rich, the so-called "bootstrappers" who had made their fortune during the boom a decade earlier. Robots, they pointed out, were more efficient, and you only had to pay for them once. Constantino generally just smiled and said he was old-fashioned, but the truth was, he owned Servo Servants, the largest robotics company in Confederate space, and he knew that you paid for them a lot more than once. Planned obsolescence and sufficiently inefficient mechanisms that required regular repairs were what kept SS in business.

Besides, he preferred to keep people employed. The more he employed, the fewer were infesting the bowels of the Gutter.

Nova glided over to him. "Daddy, you're always going on about how wonderful the servants are—but you never let them partake."

"I beg your pardon?" Naturally, if he was thinking about the servants, Nova would know that, even if only subconsciously, and talk about them with him.

"They're people too, Daddy—and they work *so* hard. Don't you think they deserve some of this fantastic Antigan buffalo a lot more than, say, *him?*"

She pointed over at Garth Duke, who had apparently decided that the punch bowl was a wading pool, and was taking off his boots. Constantino looked around, but Boris was already making a beeline before Garth could make a scene. *Or, rather, more of one.*

"Well?"

Turning back to look at his daughter, he found himself unable to resist her pleading green eyes. It wasn't the first time she had begged an indulgence for the servants, and she usually got what she asked for—a weakness of her father's that she hadn't taken nearly as much advantage of as she might have. Eleftheria said once that her telepathy probably allowed her to think of the servants as *people* rather than servants, since they had thoughts just like everyone else.

Nova herself didn't know this, of course. She simply imagined herself to be a very perceptive young woman.

He reached across to cup her cheek in his hand. "My darling girl—you know I can deny you nothing." He turned around and activated the microfone built into the button of his suit jacket.

Amplifiers placed discreetly throughout the room carried his voice over the partygoing din. "May I have everyone's attention, please?" As the room started to slowly quiet down, he grabbed two glasses of wine off the tray of a passing server and handed one to his daughter.

"Today is the fifteenth birthday of my beautiful daughter, November Annabella Terra. She is the last of our children to reach that age, and indeed the last of our children." He tipped his glass toward where Bella stood, her arm in that of her jig, and she was kind enough to return the gesture and provide an almost-genuine smile. "But being younger than her sister Clara or her brother Zebediah does not make her inferior or any less loved. Indeed, the day she was born was one of the four happiest days of my life, the other three being when her siblings were born—and, of course, when Continental went out of business, granting me a monopoly on holocams."

Ripples of laughter at the admittedly mediocre joke spread throughout the room. Nova just glared at her father, apparently not appreciating the humor. Or maybe she just didn't like it when Constantino used her full name.

"In any case, because that day made me so happy, it pleases me more than I can say that all you good people are here today to celebrate that day's anniversary. So I ask you all to raise your glasses and wish my darling Nova a happy birthday."

Everyone in the room did so, and the words were spoken raggedly throughout. Nova smiled and her cheeks flushed.

After everyone had drunk, Nova loved at Constantino and said, "Daddy!"

"Of course, my dear. And now, I'd like to ask everyone to please step back from the food and drink tables for a time. My household servants have worked hard for weeks to get this party ready, and have worked even harder to keep things running smoothly now that it's begun. So as a reward and to show my great appreciation, I invite all the servants to come forward and partake of this magnificent spread."

Several chuckles spread throughout, and a smattering of applause. Constantino noticed that most of the patrons were less amused. In particular, Bella looked like someone had poisoned her drink. And many of the patrons looked unhappy at having to move aside for servants.

Nova, however, beamed at him with a radiant smile. Turning around, he saw that Eleftheria was favoring him with a similar smile. Those were the only two reactions Constantino cared about.

A moment later, Zeb came sidling up to his father. "Dad, did you *have* to use my full name?"

Nova rolled her eyes. "Don't be such a baby, Zeb."

"Oh, that's funny. I suppose you liked him calling you 'November,' huh, *little* sister?"

"I'm fifteen years old, and I'm taller than you."

Constantino chuckled again. "He's got you there, son." Nova was already taller than both her siblings, and almost as tall as her father, and he doubted she was done growing yet.

Zeb shrugged it off. "That's just the clothes."

"You just keep telling yourself that, 'big' brother."

"Mr. Terra!"

Constantino whirled around to see Lia Emmanuel. Constantino himself was the president of every one of Terra's business ventures, with the individual day-to-day left to assorted vice presidents. Lia was the vice president in charge of the vice presidents, as it were, and Constantino counted on her as his right hand in all matters relating to his many and varied businesses.

She was dressed in the same suit she always wore. Lia had twelve identical suits, and wore a different one each day, laundering them when time permitted or when twelve days passed, whichever came first. Constantino doubted she owned any other clothes—which was a pity, as she was the only one in the room in business attire. Everyone else was wearing a much more celebratory brand of formalwear.

Moving away from the sibling argument—which would probably keep going for at least another five to ten minutes—Constantino approached his vice president. "Lia—haven't seen you all night. Where've you—?"

"Sir, I'm sorry, we need to talk." Lia stared at him intently with her piercing brown eyes. Her curly brown hair was tied sloppily atop her head, as if she just wanted to get it out of her way as quickly as possible. "In private."

Constantino sighed. "Why didn't you simply buzz me?"

Lia's stare intensified into a glare. "Because you turned your fone off and left it in your bedroom, sir."

"Imagine that," Constantino said dryly. "You'd think I was throwing a party that I didn't want interrupted by business."

Now Lia winced. "I'm sorry, sir, truly, and I wouldn't have interrupted Nova's party normally, but—"

Again, Constantino sighed. It was true, Lia would never have been so gauche as to have business intrude upon family like this unless it was urgent. "All right, all right, what is it?"

"Rebels, sir. They've attacked and destroyed the plant in Palombo Valley."

Constantino blinked. "Destroyed? The *entire* plant?"

"Effectively, sir. I believe some of the structure is still intact, but the plant is functionally useless at present, sir. This will set back production of the 878 and 901 hover-cars and especially the 428 hoverbikes by—"

Waving it off, Constantino said, "I don't care about that right now, Lia—how many people—"

"The entire night shift, sir. The ID tag scans of the wreckage matches all but three of the night-shift employees, and of those three, one was on vacation and the other two called in sick. Everyone else is dead. DNA verification will take another hour, but we're pretty sure—"

"I want all three of them investigated—find out if they're collaborators." Constantino let out a breath through his teeth, trying to rein in his temper. It wouldn't do to cause a scene here, especially with so much of his competition present.

"That's already under way, sir. The attack was such that it *had* to be an inside job. The bombs used were very specifically targeted to the areas of the plant that either would be most densely populated during the night shift or would have the equipment that would be most expensive to replace."

Knowing this was a stupid question—who else would do this sort of thing, after all?—Constantino nonetheless had to ask, "We're sure it's rebels?"

Lia nodded. "Completely sure, sir. Mengsk did one of his pirate broadcasts at the same time as the attack, condemning the Old Families in general and you in particular as symptomatic of the decay that has gripped—"

Again, he interrupted, not caring about Mengsk's propaganda. "All right, fine. Keep on it, and prepare a full report. I'll read it when the party's over." He sighed. "Dammit. This was a good evening, too."

"Sir, the news gets worse. I've run the financials and—well, you can either rebuild the plant or you can give bereavement pay to the families of the victims. You can't do both."

"Then we'll put off rebuilding the plant," Constantino said without hesitation, "we—"

"Sir, we were counting on that plant to produce enough vehicles, especially the 428s, to counteract last year's falloff."

Sales of most Terra products had flattened out of late, due in part to an economic downturn, in part to fear of rebel attacks driving down consumer spending. The one exception to this was the 428 model of hoverbike, which was incredibly popular among both children and younger adults.

Lia continued: "We can stave off maybe a few months, but we *have* to get that plant back up and running right away. Mengsk didn't choose it randomly—he knew that without that plant, our ability to get back into the black will be next to impossible without—"

"Without screwing over the families of the victims of his attack." Constantino shook his head. "Bastard. If we don't rebuild, we start falling apart. If we do rebuild, we give him more fodder for his crap about how we exploit the workers." He had to resist the urge to spit. "Dammit. All right, Lia, thanks."

"Sir, I'm afraid—"

"I'm not going to make a decision about that now."

"Sir, that's not what I need to tell you about. There's more bad news—the Protoss have wiped out Mar Sara.

The Confederacy managed to pull back, but I'm not sure how many got out alive."

Constantino shook his head. He knew the experiments being done on the Zerg they'd captured in the Sara system would come back to haunt them all. They'd already wiped out Chau Sara, and now Mar Sara had gone the same way. And who knew where these Protoss bastards would stop?

"Thank you, Lia. We'll talk after the party, all right?"

"Yes, sir." She turned on her heel and headed for the lift.

Looking down at his left hand, Constantino saw that he still had the glass of wine in it. Aside from the sip he took for Nova's toast, he hadn't touched it.

Now he swallowed it all in one gulp. The fruity taste almost made up for the sting of the alcohol as it plunged down his throat faster than wine was intended to be drunk, but right at the moment, Constantino didn't care all that much.

Eleftheria intercepted him on his way back to Nova and Zeb. As was often the case with mistresses, Eleftheria was the opposite of Constantino's wife. Where Bella was a short, stout brunette with olive skin and an hourglass figure, Eleftheria was a tall, willowy redhead with pale skin and a slim figure.

"That was Lia. She came late, talked to you for two seconds, then immediately left. That usually adds up to bad news."

"No flies on you, m'dear." He chuckled without mirth. Eleftheria had always been observant. He told her about what happened to the Palombo plant—he couldn't tell her about the Protoss. That was something she wasn't cleared to be aware of, much as it pained him to keep anything from her.

Eleftheria's already-pale face grew paler. "My God, that's awful. How could they *do* that?"

"Apparently, we *all* have to pay for the sins of the Council's idiotic decisions." Constantino had been the loudest among those arguing furiously against the bombing of Korhal IV as too extreme a solution, but many of the Old Families took the Council's side—as well as that of the military—in believing that extreme problems *demanded* extreme solutions.

Except that Constantino and his allies had been correct. Korhal IV had backfired rather spectacularly, turning public opinion further away from the Confederacy. And the bombing gave rise to Mengsk and his band of butchers, not to mention dozens of other smaller rebellious groups who didn't have Mengsk's profile, but were irritants just the same.

He looked over at Nova and Zeb, now talking more civilly to each other. *Lia said it was an inside job. Maybe one of the three who were out. Maybe one of the corpses in the plant, willing to be a martyr for Mengsk's cause.*

"What are you thinking?" Eleftheria asked.

"That we're going ahead with the plan." He put down the wineglass and grabbed another glass from a passing server.

His mistress's eyes went wide. "I thought you said—"

"I said I was considering abandoning it, but this attack makes it imperative." *Not to mention what just happened in the Sara system.* "If they can get someone inside the plant, they can get someone inside this household." He smiled grimly. "Security's a lot more stringent for my businesses than it is for my home, I'm afraid." He took a sip of the wine. This was an inferior vintage to the previous one. *We must have run out of the '09. This tastes like the '07.* As he recalled, the grape crop on Halcyon was awful that year. He made a mental note to ask the wine steward why they had any of that vintage in the wine rack at all.

Eleftheria asked, "But if one of the household staff was untrustworthy, Nova would know, wouldn't she?"

"Not necessarily. She's not trained, she doesn't know what to look for." *And whose fault is that?* a little voice in his head asked, but Constantino tamped it down. The only way to get that training was to lose his daughter altogether, and that he *would* not do—not to the very same imbeciles who nuked Korhal IV and started this entire nonsense.

"When are you going to tell her?" Eleftheria asked.

"After the party. Let her have a good time tonight—then I'll tell her that she's going to have to go offworld for a while."